DOC AND HER DRAGON

UP SHIFT CREEK BOOK 2: A F.U.C. ACADEMY STORY

JULIA MILLS

CONTENTS

An EveL Worlds Production : www.worlds.EveLanglais.com

AUTHOR'S NOTE

And we're back! Can you believe it? Eve let me write a second book in the amazing FUCN'A World. Not only are Freddie and Buck from *A Tree Frog and Her Honey Badger* back, but this story is also about their besties—Del and Matt.

Yes! It's true! The Up Shift Creek Gang is back, and things are hairier than ever! Doc and Her Dragon brings in some of the old gang, some new characters, and a whole lotta messed-up fun that you just don't wanna miss.

I sure hope you enjoy Doc and Her Dragon and all the stories in this amazing EveL world created by the one and only Eve Langlais.
Stay Safe. Take Care. And ALWAYS Dare to Dream!

XOXO, Julia

ACKNOWLEDGMENTS

Thank you to:

- my proofreader, Book Nook Nuts
- beta readers Charlene Bauer and Jessica Ripley
- EveL Worlds editor Devin Govaere, and
- cover artist Rebecca Poole with Dreams2Media!

To Liz and Em, you are my world. Beautiful women, inside and out, who make every day a blessing. I am so proud of you. Being your mom is the best thing that ever happened to me!

To anyone out there who truly understands the saying, All the Planning in the World Can't Beat Dumb Luck, this story is for you!

To Jess Ripley—Lady, I do not know what I would do without you. Never stop being you, 'cause the world might just stop turning. LOVE YOU!

INTRODUCTION

A dragon king and a dragonfly take on an icy-hot salamander in this next addition to the FUCN'A world!

Take one doctor with a glittering green body, sparkly wings, and a sassy alter-ego who refuses to take no for an answer. Add an explosives professor with red scales and a heart of gold who shares his soul with an ancient dragon king.

Mix in the most FUCN'A band of amazing friends a couple could ask for, and you've got a story like no other that will have you laughing, cheering, and falling in love till the very end!

Doc and Her Dragon are out to solve the conundrum of a seriously deranged and absolutely deceased mega-lomaniac and psychopath who is posthumously trying to turn the shifters of the world into super dino super soldiers.

Stop right there! You're about to be FUC'd—in the best possible way, and that's just the beginning!

Does this premise and world seem familiar? That's because it is based off Eve Langlais' Furry United Coalition. Eve has invited her author friends to come and play in her world! To find out more, visit worlds.EveLanglais.com.

Chapter 1

"Ready?"

"Hell, no, I'm not ready!"

"Set?"

"Are you deaf? Your ears broken? Pay attention! If I'm not ready, I'm damned sure not set! Maybe we should—"

"Shut up and go for it!"

Screaming at the top of her lungs, more freaked out than she'd ever been in her whole entire life, Del refused to be denied. There was no way she would stop. They'd come too far to back down. The answer had to be just seconds away. She could feel it in the sparkles on her wings—just one more try. One last, more contained, and—hopefully—less devastating explosion, and they would finally be able to help.

Goddess knew they'd blown up more than one—three to be exact—shed, four derelict cars, and one rotten tree stump in the middle of the woods trying to find the right concoction to help the poor professor. Del's best friend would just have to get a grip. This final experiment, the culmination of six months' work, was happening. And that was that.

Dr. Delilah F. Weathersbee, preeminent physician to all beings supernatural, paranormal, and just plain weird, continued her war cry as she dashed across the abandoned warehouse as fast as her feet would carry her. No doubt that her wings would've been quicker, but singe marks on their glittery tips would've been a serious fashion faux pas and just another reason for her alter ego to bitch and moan.

"No shit, I'd be bitchin' and moanin'. Even one spec of burning ash hits my beautifully perfect wings—"

"Shut up," Del internally snapped to the voice in her head. *"I'm using my feet. Even you can see that. I'll argue with you in a min—"*

"Not good enough, Delilah Flashwing Weathersbee! Not good enou—"

"Del, dammit. My name is Del. You're not my mother or my granny or—"

"I'll call you whatever I damned well want to call you. I'm the one stuck in your brain, subjected to the unimaginable cruelty of that ever-thinking, always whirring mind of yours. Some of the shit you dream up should be outlawed. Hell, it probably has been in all fifty states and every province, territory, and backass forest in Canada."

Surama—Suri for short—Flashwing-Sparks, Princess of the Blue Empress Dragonflies of South America, kept right on going before Del could so much as sneak a syllable in edgewise. *"And while I'm at it, I swear to all that's holy and anything unholy that happens to be listening, if I end up* truly *dead... You know what I'm talking about. The never to return, no longer breathing, my wings cease to flutter, and I'm yuckily buried in some pile of dirt in the middle of nowhere after nineteen-hundred-and-seventy years on this earth, deceased, D-E-C-E-A-S-E-D... You. Will. Pay. I promise to do a body snatch on the gravedigger and make him dig up your smelly, decomposing corpse before the tip of your nose even has time to turn the lightest color of blue."*

"How can my nose not be blue if I'm already smelly and decomposing?"

"Shut up with the science BS. I get enough of that shit already. I'm on a roll! Once the gravedigger recovers your corpse, I'll have that voodoo doctor from NOLA with the sexy ass and dark brown eyes—the one you wouldn't let me get my feelers on because you're so mean to me—reanimate your butt with the ugliest, most grotesque little pile of rotten chicken bones and lizard hearts he can find."

"What does the condition of the chicken bones and lizard hearts have to do with anything?" Del kept right on talking as she checked to be sure Freddie was still tucked safely behind their barricade.

"Oh, they are an integral part. Were you sleeping in Rituals of the Occult 101 in primary school? Don't answer. I know you weren't. Hush up and pay attention. I'm threatening you here. At least have the decency to pretend to be scared."

"Don't have time," Del panted, gasping for breath

because running was just not her thing unless there was a bottle of good zinfandel involved or a special lecture live stream on new medical techniques for the removal of silver from the ass of a screeching baboon shifter. *"Gotta... Gotta get this.... this..."*

"Just keep those little tootsies movin' and listen, Del, this may be the largest warehouse ever built in the history of good, old Canadian engineering—"

"Wouldn't that be Canadian construction? Or architecture? Or—"

"Or maybe you should shut up and pour on the speed?" Suri's deadpan sarcasm almost made Del laugh. *"Keep movin', Sista. Run, Del, Run. It's the least you can do. Now, where was I? Oh yeah... Then, just because you'll most assuredly deserve it for causing my untimely and definitely devastating-for-the-world demise, I'll haunt you for the rest of forever by singing 'Girls Just Wanna Have Fun' at the top of my lungs."*

Getting a second wind, or maybe it was simply her inability to allow Suri to have the last word, Del retaliated with her alter ego's full name. *"You better be careful there, Princess Surama Flashwing-Sparks. Your mouth's writin' checks your ass can't cash. Your people don't have a good history with mouthing off and throwing bullshit around like its Mardi Gras beads. You might want to think about—"*

"Oh, see here now," Suri snarled. *"There you go again. Bringin' up my ancestors, throwing past mistakes in my face. Mistakes, I might add, that happened before I was even born. Besides, if it hadn't been for dear old great-great-great-great-great-and-then-some-grandpa running into that*

coyote and taking that stupid bet, you might not even be here. Ever think of that, Delilah, my girl?"

"Yeah, I thought about it. Pretty much the same way I'm thinkin' this frikkin' building is getting bigger with every step I take. Are you doin' this? Are you tryin' to kill me? It will not be natural causes if I die of a dragonfly-alter-ego-induced cardiac arrest," Del huffed and panted. *"They'll know it was your fault. The coroner will be sure to put that on the death certificate."*

"Shut up and run, De. Just shut up and run."

Okay, so the pompous, arrogant, extremely loveable, and utterly irreplaceable dragonfly princess with whom the doctor shared her soul was right, but that didn't mean Del was going to give her the satisfaction of admitting it. Nope. No way. No how. Not when they were in the middle of a heated argument, the physician was sprinting so fast it felt like her hair was on fire, and she knew there was about to be one hell of a *boom.*

Yes, the creation of the dragonfly shifters—no matter how strange and unusual—had been an absolutely fantastic twist of fate and kismet. It was a weird blast of destiny that both formidable and amazing ladies absolutely and without a doubt believed was the coolest thing to ever happen. After all, had Suri's grandpa—referred to by everyone in the know as "the old king"—not made the biggest mistake of his life all those hundreds of thousands of years ago, the dragonfly shifters might have never been born. Worse still, the looney and loveable Doc and her dragonfly might never have shared a soul, never shared hour upon hour upon hour of sassy banter, never-ending teasing, and incomparable bonding. Hell, Del might never have gone into medicine, gone to work for the FUC, and, goddess forbid, never met Matt.

There was no denying the fact that they were more than human and dragonfly—they were sisters. Their joining was the silver lining on what would always sit in the top three most incredible fuckups of all time.

But that didn't mean that Del was going to let Suri have the satisfaction of being right. She couldn't ever let that happen. It just wasn't her style. She couldn't keep her comments—or thoughts—to herself. Especially not after being challenged.

"Yeah, well, it wasn't one of my relatives who was dumb enough to be tricked by a coyote. You'd think a dragon king would know better than to listen to some mangy, flea-bitten mongrel in the middle of the desert."

"Yeah, well, don't get me started. Your people have a long and illustrious history of fuckups. I've lived through most of them. Y'all aren't perfect. Humans have just as many skeletons in their closets, and not one of them has scorch marks on their wings. Just keep that shit to your—"

"Oh, will you puh-lease chill?" Del sassed. *"I know what I'm doing. I always know what I'm doing. Except when I don't, and that hasn't happened in years. I mean, come on. Have I gotten you killed yet?"*

"No, but there's a first time for everything."

"Just trust me, will ya?"

"Famous last words of every man, woman, and alter-ego whose autopsy ever said: died under stupidly suspicious

circumstances. My tombstone is gonna read: Here lies Suri. She told Del not to do it, but the crazy chick wouldn't listen."

"Ignoring you now."

And that was precisely what she did. The Doc had bigger fish to fry. Being with Suri since the day of her birth, Del had invented a mystical, magical, make-believe Princess Surama-specific mute button in her head.

Sliding to a stop, she panted so hard the huge plastic safety goggles covering her bright green eyes fogged up worse than the windshield of her bright red Mini Cooper, Matilda, in the dead of winter. Praying with all her might for a steady hand and good aim, Del reached forward as far as her arms would go.

"Goddess, be with me," she whispered. "Just please don't let me vaporize the whole planet." She tossed the pahoehoe lava into the bubbling beaker—her last ten grams from the Potrillo Volcanic Fields in the middle of the Chihuahua Desert.

"Feet don't fail me now," she added.

Up on her toes and spinning to the right, Del swung her arms backward with all her might before jerking them forward as high as they would go. Holding her breath and using the momentum of her whipping appendages like they were her very own wings, the doc launched herself into the air like she'd been shot out of a cannon. Aiming for somewhere—*anywhere*—behind the pile of sandbags, cracked concrete blocks, and the metric shit-ton of broken furniture and pallets she and her best friend—aka partner-in-crime—were calling the "wall of doom," Del closed her eyes tight and flew through the air with less than the greatest of ease.

Landing with a thud, just barely keeping her ass from crashing onto the cracked and crumbling cement floor, she shrieked the countdown Freddie always insisted they use. "Three… two…one…"

But that was as far as she got, her mind working overtime to find the miscalculation causing the "early ejaculation of explosives," as *Crash! Boom! Bang!* and *Ka-blooey* ensued with all the vim and vigor of a seven-point-three earthquake.

Not only did the ringing in her ears sound like the bells of St. Mary's on Easter morning, but tears rivaling the rapids of Niagara Falls ran down her cheeks as noxious green fumes filled the air. Hands instinctually flying over her head, she made a makeshift umbrella to protect her long auburn locks from the crackling chartreuse crud raining down all around.

"This shit is awesome," she breathed, marveling as the sizzling sparkles, the color of shamrocks, incinerated everything they touched.

"Yeah, sure, if you like fire," Freddie grumbled before adding with a chuckle, "Which I frikkin' do. Almost as much as I love my coffee and my man."

"Hell, yeah," Del screamed over the chaos. "That should be a shirt. *Things to do today: (1) Get Out of bed. (2) Find Coffee. (3) Blow Shit Up.*"

'You make it. I'll wear it," Freddie yelled, followed by a maniacal cackle that made Del grin from ear to ear.

The chemical reaction was nothing short of cataclysmic and catastrophic and absolutely fantastic to watch.

Not only was science Del's thing, but impressive explosions with all the trimmings were the whipped cream, sprinkles, and cherry on top of her already stupendous scientific sundae. There wasn't a soul alive who didn't know that solving the unsolvable with loud booms was Dr. Delilah Weatherbee's thing. Hell, even the Universe was onboard.

The almighty, omnipotent Being in charge of *absolutely everything* made the perfect mate for the renowned doctor in none other than Matthew Firestone. The man was sexy as all get-out. Not only did he have red hair a couple of shades darker than her own, but those gorgeous brown eyes made Del weak in the knees, his muscles made her fingers tingle with the need to touch, and, damn it all, his heart was as pure as the driven snow.

Best of all, and almost as important, Matthew Firestone was a Dragon Guardsman with a penchant for fire. Talk about a perfect fit for his profession as the professor of Advanced Explosives, Bomb Making in the Trenches with Whatever's in Your Pocket, and Let Detonators be Your Friend at FUCN'A—that was the Furry United Coalition Newbie Academy, the best training grounds for shifter agents looking for a life in protecting shifters and the shifter secret from all humankind.

Talk about a match made in Heaven. That man was

perfect for Del in every single way and doubly magnificent in all the ways that really counted.

There was only one problem. Del's red dragon shifter with a heart of gold, the best ass the good goddess ever fashioned, and the ability to kiss her senseless continually "requested" that she not blow things up when he wasn't there to put out the fire. However, the doc refused to be denied. When she and her bestie, Dr. Winifred—please call her Freddie—Lightfoot-Blackthorne—were working on a problem, all bets were off. They lost track of time, forgot what day it was, and always, without a doubt, set something ablaze.

If it took blowing up burlap bags stuffed with hay to resemble the bad guys to figure out if a new, experimental chemical concoction could be used as ammo in the field, they were all in. If detonating bombs filled with the magical, mystical hallucinogenic fog only Dr. Weathersbee—in her dragonfly form—could shoot from her heinie to solve the problem at hand, they went for it with wild abandon. Setting up a bunch of Bunsen burners, test tubes, and connecting them with a hundred or so feet of flexible plastic pipes was never out of the question. Neither was blowing up every beaker in FUCN'A and covering the walls with radioactive goo, then begging for forgiveness long after the fact. Suffice it to say, these ladies, doctors, supernatural shifters were the ones to get the job done.

However, on this occasion, more than curiosity was at stake. Del and Freddie's numerous experiments—

every single one to date ending in detonations, explosions, and plumes of technicolor smoke—were being executed for the best reason either woman had ever seen: the consummation of blessed matehood for their new bestie.

Yep! The truth was stranger than fiction. The newest member of their tribe—coined the Ladies of Disaster by their significant others—a certain Rhode Island Red Hen named Dusty had found the one man in all the universe made for her. The yin to her yang, the peanut butter to her marshmallow cream, the bow-chica to her wow-wow. The airplane mechanic, ex-marine, and best friend to Buck—Freddie's mate—was nothing short of spectacular. Not only did she save the couple from inevitable demise at the hands of a psycho yellowjacket, but along the way, Dusty found her mate, and that made the Rhode Island Red numero uno times two in Del's book.

The problem was said hunka-hunka dino hotness was stuck in a genetically engineered nightmare and unwilling to commit—or even so much as kiss the blonde-haired blue-eyed hen—as long as he looked like the supervillain from a Saturday morning cartoon. If this wasn't a riddle for the renowned—and sometimes infamous, most definitely notorious as far as their boss was concerned—Teacher in Tight Spaces, then nothing was. They would get to the bottom of it and change that dino back to a dude, or their names weren't Del and Freddie.

Back on her feet, with her bestie at her side, Dr. Del,

as she was known to everyone at FUCN'A, pointed the nozzle of the super-sized, heavy-duty fire extinguisher she'd liberated from the Advanced Explosives Lab—without asking her dragon—at the largest of the lime green flames. Hitting the lever with the index finger of her left hand, she watched as the fetid fumes of her failed experiment were spewed into submission with purple foam that sadly smelled way too much like the foot cream she'd whipped up to remove fairy warts from her dad's big toes.

"What the hell are we gonna do now?" she yelled over the hiss and pop of the pastel popcorn flames jumping around as if they'd been thrown into a pan of hot oil. "How are we gonna tell Dusty that we can't change Dino Dave back to the man he once was? Or that we used up all the lava crystals from the last active desert volcano in the whole damned world? I mean, it's not like you can order magically infused lava crystals that can only be created with the one remaining rainbird of legend blows up the mythical baddie known as the Psônen from any sight on Ghougle. Hell, there's no prime delivery for crap like that, is there? We only knew about them because Matt is friends with the MacAllens." Holding up her index finger to keep her bestie from interrupting, the doc added, "Or, and this is the worst of all, for the first time in forever, we can't come up with an answer?"

"First of all..." Freddie corrected, her right eyebrow arched as high as it would go as she stopped spraying fire extinguisher goo all over the smoldering ash in favor of facing Del. "You're lucky my coffee is over there on the window sill in an airtight thermos of my own design."

"Oh, crap," Del tried not to laugh at her friend's all-encompassing love of java. "Thank the Goddess for small favors."

"You know it," the winged tree frog harrumphed. "And almost as importantly…"

"Hit me." The doc nodded. "Dazzle me with your brilliance. I know you got something cooking in that kickass brain of yours. Even without a gallon or so of coffee racing through your veins, you never let me down."

"Hold on to your hat, my friend," Freddie assured, the sweet scent of her confidence filling the air between them. "We're gonna stop calling my friend and mentor Dino Dave and start using the name his momma gave him—Dr. Alexander Anatoli. After all, I had to vouch for him with my word of honor, Buck's ass, and on the life of our first born—if that ever happens."

"Oh, it'll happen," Del snickered, not surprised that her friend kept right on talking.

"Miranda and Chase were ready to lock his scaly ass up in a dino-sized prison with reinforced bars in the deepest pit they could dig in the Canadian outback. Thank all the little fishies in the ugly green Swamp they believed me when I told them that the dino-spider-mane wolf hybrid standing before them was really an ancient dino shifter who also happened to be my old professor."

"And mine," Del chimed in. "I swear, I wish we could get that voodoo doctor Suri has a crush on to reanimate Zenobia just so I could kick her ass, too."

"We really need to look into that," Freddie nodded, her eyes big and her brow furrowed. "But until we get him fixed, we really need to call Alexander by his real name. If for no other reason than to remind him who he is and make sure he knows that we're trying everything possible to get him back to normal."

"Yeah, you're right. It's just so frikkin' confusing. I mean, it's clear the professor's brain still works just fine. That's glaringly obvious every time he opens his mouth. All that gorgeous intelligence is still there, but I wanna stop seeing him in my clinic, ya know? I just can't help that I see Barney after an acid trip every time I look at him. It's more than a little freaky, ya know? He's a dinosaur with a mohawk and a tattoo on his forearm, with wolf fur covering most of his skin and venomous pincher-fangs sticking out of his snout. It's a challenge not to look like a deer in the headlights whenever he shows up."

"Well, hell, maybe—"

"No, no, no." Del furiously shook her head. "I can deal. I. Will. Deal. As long as we can put things back the way they should be. I just wanna help. Not only for Dino…I mean Alexander, but Dusty. She's done so much for all of us. She's just the best. Nobody deserves to be happy as much as she does."

“Damn, girl, you’ve got one helluva turn of phrase.” Freddie laughed out loud. “Barney after an acid trip? Did you just pull that shit outta your ass, or you been savin' that little gem for just the right moment?"

"Just came to me right this minute," Del proudly chuckled. "See? Told ya. I still got all the moves."

“Ya damned sure do, and you echoed exactly what I was thinking. Alexander is as brilliant as he always was. The exterior's just different, and it's one he hates. It makes him feel less than, and that sucks. Hell, he taught me damned near everything I know about paleontology and archeology, and…"

"And that's sayin' something." Del chuckled, releasing the trigger on her own fire extinguisher when the last of the lime green flames flickered out. "Cause you're one smart cookie, Delly girl."

"Thanks, girl. Right back atcha."

"And you've said those exact words at least a hundred-and-seventy-two times in the last six months and thought I ignored all of ’em.”

"You've been counting?" Freddie tried acting pissed before breaking out in giggles. "I knew you had my back." With a swish of her free hand and her finger jabbing at the air between them in time with her words, she jumped right back to the subject at hand, reminding Del why she loved the princess of the winged tree frog shifters like a sister. "Is it his fault he was the only ancient dino shifter still alive with two parents who were also full-blooded dino shifters? No. Did he have any idea that the bitch of all bitches had a fiendish plan to kidnap his butt and use his precious DNA to not only fuck with him but also turn every shifter she could grab off the streets into her own army of mutant super soldiers?" Index finger pointing at the ceiling, she gave a single emphatic shake of her head. "No and no."

Not missing a beat or, for that matter, taking a breath, Del smirked in amazement at Freddie's ability to keep her train of thought and continue talking. "And to answer your question, we're not telling our dear buddy, Dusty, one damned thing. Not just yet. No way. Not gonna happen. Not if we can help it, or it's the very last resort. I distinctively remember telling you and anyone who would listen that without Zenobia Petalblast's notes—you know the ones that were blown to smithereens when she torched her whole underground hive—we'd never—"

"Yep, I remember. You said, without that data, a snowball had a better chance of surviving Hell than we did of reverse engineering whatever she did to Dino Dave, I mean Alexander. But…"

"But nothing, Del," the winged tree frog shifter cut in, her free hand waving in the air between them. "Zenobia was a witch with a capital B. She literally made my ass twitch in ways an ass should never twitch, but that crazy Queen Bee was smart, and the crap she did to Alex and all the others was just… just… just a load of bullshit and a sin against nature."

"Hell yeah!" Del roared, throwing her fist in the air.

"And she ain't no smarter than us. We don't need her shit. There's an answer, and we're gonna find it."

"Hell yeah! We don't need her shit. Can't get it anyway."

Happy her bestie echoed the doc's cheer with a wave of her own fist, Del knew there was more to come and could barely wait to hear what it was as Freddie added, "And I have a plan."

"Now that's what I like to hear. Tell me. Tell me."

"How do you feel about a trip south of the border?"

"Do you mean what I think you mean?"

"You know it and then some." Waving the first two fingers of her left hand between them, she winked. "They don't call us the Ladies of Disaster for nuthin'."

"But we've already been to the desert and used all of the only two-hundred grams of the pahoehoe ash we could find. What's going back there gonna—"

"Oh, pa-hooey-hooey and kiss my booty. I—"

"It's pronounced *puh-howee-howee*."

"Yeah, well, that didn't work with my rhyme," Freddie grumbled. "Don't mess with my flow, Delly girl." Winking and grinning before charging full steam ahead, the most brilliant winged tree frog to ever keep her butt from bumping on the ground when she hopped confidently announced, "We're not going back to the desert for stupid lava or ash, baby. Not even for Zenobia's notes, which we know aren't there. We're heading south of the border to meet with an honest-to-the-goddess living, breathing person... Well, shifter. The only one I know who can help."

"Okay, great swami with the mystical powers to create people outta thin air, how we gonna get there? The last time you said anything about your plane…"

"The Lightfoot-Blackthorne FUC-U 2.0, Del. Call her by her name. She hears all and knows all and needs to be recognized for her tremendous and unfathomable contributions."

"Yeah, her." Del nodded, her free hand waving forward, backward, and up and down because talking with her hands helped her think. "The Lightfoot-Blackthorne, yadda, yadda, yadda…"

"Close enough." Freddie laughed. "Proceed."

"Why, thank you, Dr. Lightfoot-Blackthorne."

"You're welcome, Dr. Weathersbee-Soon-to-be-Firestone." Freddie giggled in response.

Just barely holding back her laughter, Del hurried to speak before her bestie could interrupt for the third time. "How are we gonna get to the desert? There is absolutely no way in heaven or hell that Director Alyce Cooper's gonna let you take another FUC plane. Hell, she won't even let you drive a golf cart across campus without supervision. Her last memo said, and I quote, 'Dr. Winifred Lightfoot-Blackthorne is forbidden from driving anything with more power than a bicycle without a partner. Our insurance company has spoken. We will be dropped and considered uninsurable by all of British Columbia, maybe the whole of Canada, and assuredly the United States.'"

"Yeah, well, little does she know that the Lightfoot-Blackthorne FUC-U 2.0 is up and running and better than ever. With a little help from FUCN'A's newest aeronautics instructor and mechanical engineer, along with a large chunk of my savings account, my baby is ready to take to the wild blue yonder and show the world what she's made of."

"Wooohooooo!" Del cheered, so thrilled that she jumped up and down and clapped her hands.

Unfortunately, in all the excitement, one of the most intelligent people in the whole damned world—and then some—forgot she was holding a huge and unbelievably powerful fire extinguisher… until it was too late. Working as hard as she could to stop the swinging motion of her hand, it was as if a switch had been flipped and the world was suddenly moving in slow motion.

There was nothing she could do. No matter how hard she tried. The momentum was just too strong.

The thought of helping her new bestie had overridden the doc's common sense and tugged at her heart. She'd forgotten all about the extinguisher. All she could do was scream, "Watch out, Freddie," and pray that her bestie understood. "Grab my coffee! Save the coffee! Imma need that sweet, sweet java after this BS!"

Sadly, that wasn't enough either.

One hand hit the other. The feel of cold stainless steel stung her palm. And her heart stopped as the trigger of the fire extinguisher was instantly, unceremoniously, and unfortunately trapped between both her hands.

Down it went. A whoosh, louder than fireworks at

the stroke of midnight on New Year's Eve, rang in her ears. Her heart stopped, and Suri screamed, *"What could go wrong? Did you really tempt that beyotch called Fate and ask what could go wrong? This! This, Del! This could go wrong. You're shooting stinky shit all over our best friend!"*

No truer words had ever been spoken. Just like that, smelly bright purple foam spewed from the end of the nozzle—and right into the midsection of Freddie Lightfoot-Blackthorne.

Spinning to the right as fast as she could, hoping she could minimize the damage, Del wailed, "Oh, my goddess! Oh, my goddess! Oh, my goddess! I'm so sorry! I'm so sorry! I'm sooooooooo sorry!" Screaming at the top of her lungs, she twisted her neck as far as it could go, her head still facing front and her eyes glued to her bestie.

True to form, Freddie was unaffected and still laughing out loud but quick for paybacks.

Moving faster than Del could track, the winged tree frog pointed the spigot of her fire extinguisher right at the dragonfly princess' butt, hit the trigger, and cackled as loud as she could. "Right back atcha, girlie!"

Tears running down her face, her sides hurting from all the laughter, and her ass covered in stinky purple goo, Del teased, "So, now that we're even, can we get the hell outta Dodge?" Raising her free hand, she gave a mock salute and a wink, adding, "First bottle of tequila's on you."

Chapter 2

"So, you ready to take the *big plunge,* Matt?" The teasing question came from J.D., one of the legendary MacAllen dragons and the professor's closest friend for as long as he could remember.

"Yeah, man." Buck Blackthorne—honey badger shifter, a six-month veteran of FUC, and Freddie Lightfoot-Blackthorne's mate—snickered, smiling and nodding his head. "Being mated is no joke. It's absolutely the best and most terrifying thing that's ever happened to me. Without my girl—"

"You'd be more of a mess than we see before us now," Mason yelled as he walked into Sam's Diner, the one and only sit-down restaurant in Valentine, Texas, and that side of the Chihuahua Desert. Not only was he Matt's younger brother, but the red dragon had just received his acceptance letter in FUCN'A, much to his brother's dismay. "Having a mate just made old Buck here more touchy-feely than he already was. A real cream puff! And let's face it, nobody needs to see that shit. Don't let the bristly honey badger bullshit fool ya. Buck's just a big, ol' marshmallow with a hard candy shell."

"Aw, man, why ya gotta tell all my secrets?"

"'Cause that's what little brothers do," Matt grumbled even as his smile grew. "Even if they're not your own. They were literally put on this earth to drive us older sibs nuts."

"Come on now," objected Chase Brownsmith, a mountain of a man, usually grumpy, but always direct, grizzly bear, FUC agent, and mate to Miranda, the fiercest saber-toothed rabbit Matt ever met. Well, to be fair, the only saber-toothed bunny Matt had ever met, but that seemed immaterial after his years of friendship with the bouncy blonde agent. "I love my brothers. No matter how big of a pain in the ass they are. But you guys are right. There's nothing better than having a mate. You guys know I don't wax poetical, but just this once, I'll admit that I love Miranda more than—"

"More than honey-baked ham, homemade honey yeast rolls, and honey pecan pie made from the Sampson family secret recipe?" asked Maggie Mae Sampson as she walked through huge double doors from the kitchen to the dining room. "With honey being the operative word," she added with a chuckle.

Matt had known the co-owner of the diner and co-alpha to the Sampson pack since he was a young

Guardsman training under the patriarch and leader of the MacAllen Family Clan, Owen. It was amazing to look around and realize that not one damn thing had changed in all those years. Maggie Mae, right along with her twin, Bonnie Sue, were the two best cooks in the entire US of A. The Sampson family recipes were famous in the shifter community. They had a specialty for every breed, creed, and race. Supes traveled far and ordered ahead to get their hands on a piece of pie, a slice of homemade bread, or a whole box of treats to last until they could get that far south again.

Catching a glimpse of a cart piled high with food, the dragon chuckled. "Damn, Maggie, you cookin' for an army?"

"Just look around," she snorted. "Y'all could eat a herd of cattle—bones and all if I remember right."

"And that's just for lunch," her twin snickered.

The smell of all the wonderful food the twin wolves had created made Matt's stomach growl again as he got closer. Laughing as Maggie Mae winked at Chase, his eyes instantly bigger than saucers and a rarely seen smile brightening his entire demeanor, the professor laughed out loud when she gave a cheeky giggle filled with appreciation. "My momma's best friend was Beverley Stephens, alpha sow for the Stephens' sloth. So, when J.D. called and said y'all were headed this way, we fired the ovens back up and got to work."

"Oh, damn," the MacAllen dragon drawled. Jumping to his feet, he grabbed the plates from Maggie Mae.

Trying not to smile as the almost too-sweet, citrusy scent of his friend's embarrassment tickled Matt's nose, J.D. hurried to explain. "I had no clue how late it'd gotten. Didn't even dawn on me that y'all would be closed. It was fuckin' crazy out there. Chasing those salamander brothers all over every mesa and mountain of that desert was nuthin' but bullshit. Those boys get worse by the minute. We've been chasing them since I was knee-high to a grasshopper."

"You were never knee-high to anything," Matt teased, barking with laughter when J.D.'s middle finger flew out from under the rim of the platter he was holding as he kept on explaining.

"They used to steal the pop bottles from behind Emma Jean's grocery store, hold them for a day or two, then go in when she wasn't working and get the cash."

"Would be impressive if it wasn't theft," Chase grumbled.

"Yeah, well, things only got worse. There was nuthin' those boys wouldn't or couldn't steal. Didn't matter if folks locked shit up, bolted stuff to the floor, or had locks up and down both sides of their doors. The St. Honoré salamanders could get in. Shit, they can make themselves as small as a flea or as big as a bull. Some of us thought they would calm down when they got older." Shaking his head, he scoffed, "No such luck. If only their old daddy was here to see them now. He'd—"

"It's their momma they better be hopin' doesn't

come back from the dead. Old Anna Mae was scary as shit when she was in a good mood." Matt remembered all too vividly.

"You are so right." J.D. nodded. "When that old salamander looked over the glasses perched on the end of her nose and talked around the stogie hangin' out of her mouth, my brothers and I all got scared. But today was just bullshit. I mean, *come on,* those boys know the Chihuahua as well as I do. It's their natural habitat. The sons of bitches kept shifting back and forth from lizard—"

"They're amphibians, not lizards."

"Shut up, Professor," J.D. teasingly growled at Matt with a twinkle in his eye as he kept right on going. "From nasty assholes to big-ass creepy-looking assholes with tails who spit flames damned near as good as I can. Then they'd get real little and slither through one hole and tunnel after another."

Giving the FUCN'A prof a side-eyed glance that made him chuckle, the MacAllen dragon didn't miss a beat. "Better? Yeah, I thought so. Anyhow, those bastards gave us a run for our money."

"And one still got away," Chase offhandedly added as he took the plates from J.D.'s hands and set them in front of his own. "After we fuel up, we're gonna need to get back out there and round him up, too. Can't leave the SOB runnin' all over the countryside stealing shit and burning down everything in sight."

Grinning from ear to ear when J.D. swatted Chase

on the shoulder with the back of his hand, Matt laughed out loud. Only the bronze dragon had the nerve to lean over, glare at the big grizzly when he was eating, and teasingly inquire, "Wanna tell me how those boys escaped from those big bad impenetrable FUC holding cells y'all are always braggin' about, big guy?"

"I… umm… well, it's just…"

Thankfully, Maggie Mae chimed in with, "Oh, leave that poor bear alone, J.D. I'm sure it's not his fault any more than it's his cute little rabbit's. I was talkin' to Buck's momma, Janice, the other day, and she said the Brownsmiths are the best the FUC's got —excluding her boy. Y'all know better than most that sometimes shit just happens. Who knows that better than you?" Handing the MacAllen dragon two more huge platters piled high with food, she added, "Here, take these plates. Fill all those tables. Goddess knows we pushed every one that isn't bolted to the floor together and left the closed sign on the door. Y'all have the whole place to yourselves."

"Damn, I'm glad you ladies love to cook." J.D. nodded. "Mom, Dad, Dax… hell, *everybody* is off at some retreat on the reservation with granddad. I thought I was doomed to eat another baloney sandwich tonight. You saved my life."

Dipping his head and glancing up at the she-wolf, MacAllen looked like he was five years old all over again. Matt vividly remembered J.D. wearing the same expression when they were young and got caught doing something they were about to get in serious trouble for.

"'Cause y'all know I have a hard time just makin' toast unless I'm cookin' on a campfire."

"That's God's honest truth." Matt laughed out loud while reaching for a honey yeast roll before Chase could eat them all. "The last time you tried to make breakfast, the Valentine Fire Department showed up with three tankers and a ladder tower truck."

"Yep, they damned sure did, and the chief told me he'd call his brother, the sheriff, and have my ass arrested for attempted arson if I ever so much as touched the knob on the stove again. Dax won't even let me grill anymore. Just because I let a spark get away and her oleander plant burned to the ground, she says I'm a fire hazard. Can you imagine? The fire horse mated to a fire-breathing dragon thinks I might burn something down? What's a guy to do? There's fire in my veins. I mean, it could happen to anybody, right?"

"Nope," Buck chimed in, waving his hand in the air with a tight grip on the roll he'd just buttered. "Nobody but you, dude. And that's the other part of mated life, Matt. Your girl will *always* call you on your shit, and she's damned near always right." Chuckling so hard his shoulders bounced, the honey badger looked back to the MacAllen dragon and added, "By the way, how *is* that fire horse of yours?"

"She's good, man." J.D.'s demeanor softened. "Damn good. The Universe knew what She was doin' when She made my mate."

"Hear, hear," Chase cheered. "That man speaks the truth. The Universe does not make mistakes. I love Miranda and our sweet little ones more than honey, but…"

Wiping the side of his hand across his furry, honey-covered chin, dark eyes twinkling as he stared at the massive plate of ham right in front of him, the grizzly chuckled. "But now, honey…the good shit like these ladies cook with… Yeah, I gotta admit that comes in a real close second. It's no wonder Sam's Diner is so legendary. Y'all Sampson wolves know how to throw down."

As the diner filled with laughter, Matt looked around at all his friends and family. It felt good to be back in Valentine, damned good. It had been so long since he'd been back. The only thing missing was Del. He really wished she'd been able to make the trip with him, at the very least to meet J.D. But he wasn't upset. Her work was just as important as his, sometimes more so. And, hell, they had forever. He'd get her out to the desert where he grew up sooner or later. Right now, it was crucial for not only Alexander Anatoli but all of shifterkin that Del and Freddie find the antidote for the psycho yellowjacket's cruel formula.

Suppose there was some way, something the team of FUC investigators missed, showing that Zenobia—the brilliant, psychotic megalomaniac and demented queen bee who'd tried to kill Freddie and Buck—had shared her serum with someone else, another power-hungry dictator wannabe who wanted to rule the world. In that case, all hell could break loose at any moment. One drop of that shit in the water supply or, goddess forbid, a running stream or tributary, and every shifter on the face of the planet would be transformed into a furry dinosaur with poisonous fangs in a matter of weeks. The antidote was the most important thing. Meeting his people could wait.

"Yeah, it's important all right, but so is getting mated," Cillian, aka Kill, the ancient Dragon King with whom Matt shared his soul, snarled. *"Your chivalry and loyalty to not only the man you knew a century ago, but all the supes everywhere, is commendable, but come on, dude. How long ya gonna wait? Didn't Freddie tell you to put a ring on it? She's our mate's best friend. The one Del confides in. That little winged tree frog would know, dontcha think? I was there. You know I was. I'm always there. I heard her be very specific. She said, in no uncertain terms, that you needed to make your mating official. Assured you that it was just what you and your mate need. So, what the hell are you waiting for?"*

"For you to stop watchin' TV. I swear to the Heavens, I liked it better when you spoke Gaelic and acted stoic and uptight with a stick up your ass all the time. That's your thing. It's who you are. It's who every other Dragon King is. This new gamer or deadhead or dipshit persona sucks. For the love of God, just chill out and revert to your Neanderthal ways."

"Nope, dude," Kill scoffed. *"Not gonna happen. I'm so cool, and you're so not. Outta step, my man, that's what you*

are. I've spoken to my boys, and we're all steppin' up our game. Gettin' with the times. You gotta..."

Continuing as if his Dragon King wasn't still speaking, Matt got louder, his voice echoing from his mind to Cillian's like he was speaking through a metaphorical megaphone on the highest setting. *"Being 'cool' with everything, callin' me 'dude,' and quoting Beyonce is just too much. You're full of shit. If the other Dragon Kings were doin' this crap, I would've heard about it. I can't be the only Guardsman being driven stark raving mad by an ancient who thinks he's a millennial or Gen Z or whatever. You're makin' me—"*

"Listen up, Matthew Firestone." Kill's Scottish brogue, thick as his Gaelic heritage, rang loud and clear. The Dragon King was making a point in a tone that demanded respect. No matter how much it pained him, Matt couldn't help but listen." *"What I am trying to do is wake you the hell up and force you to make a move in the right direction, ya eejit. You, my lad, are not getting any younger."*

"I resent the age comment, and I have," the Guardsman stressed, realizing that Kill's words might be right on the mark but refusing to give his alter ego the satisfaction of admitting it.

With his nerves trying to get the best of him with every exchanged word, Matt faltered for just a split second as he added, *"Haven't I?"*

"No. No. No*! You have not,"* the Dragon King roared. *"Yes, you have wined and dined her. Wooed her. Been the perfect gentleman and then some. Opened doors, held out her*

chair, told her how beautiful she was every time you laid eyes on her...."

Making a show of clearing his throat like a CEO addressing the board of directors, Kill's eyes flashed a bold cerulean deep within the Guardsman's mind's eye. Tiny droplets of sweat trickled down Matt's spine as the knowledge that the Dragon King was about to drive his point home became glaringly obvious.

Though hurrying to stop whatever Kill was about to say, sadly, as usual, the Guardsman just wasn't quick enough.

"... went so far as to buy Princess Delilah Weathersbee of the Blue Empress Dragonflies of South America flowers and jewelry—all but a ring, may I point out with great emphasis —and treated her like the amazing lady she is in bed—"

"Stop right there," Matt ordered, his mind clearing as his compounding irritation crashed into the rising tide of dread. *"I will not discuss my love life—"*

"Or lack thereof."

"With you, Kill. Not now. Not ever. We had a deal. Even shook on it. No voyeurism. It's just gross. You're supposed to recede to the farthest corner of my mind, put on your magical headphones, and watch reruns of Welcome Back, Kotter.*"*

"And I did," Kill shot right back, indignation and disgust filling his tone. *"This dragon gets his lovin' the old-fashioned way, or he doesn't get it at all. Sadly, that's the way the shit goes these days. You need to check yourself before you wreck yourself, Matty, my man. If you don't want me to know what you do and don't do, you better lock down*

those sexy thoughts and stop relivin' every steamy detail of your and the doc's sexy times. Some days it's like a Penthouse *highlight reel up in here."*

Gone was the stoic Dragon King of old. Back was the deadhead wannabe. Any other time it would be the last straw of the already crumbling camel's back, but this time, none of it mattered.

No sooner had Kill's words floated through Matt's mind than images of his gorgeous dragonfly flashed to life. Almost as vivid as the real thing, absolutely just as beautiful, Dr. Delilah Weathersbee was the only woman Matt had ever loved. The only woman he *would* ever love. That amazing female completed the Guardsman in ways he'd never known possible. Del was his everything. She was the other half of his soul, the light to his dark, the reason for every beat of his heart.

From the first moment he'd laid eyes on her, there'd never been a doubt. Sure, it took him longer than most to make his move, but his full-time service commitment to the Dragon Guard was in full swing. He was on assignment, investigating a case closely tied to the Furry United Coalition. Not only his commander and mentor, Carrick of the Golden Fire Clan, but Kloe Manners, FUC mission director, had been very specific —no fraternization with any members of FUC, including the teachers, doctors, and other academy staff, until the case was closed.

Of course, meeting Del on his first day at FUCN'A lit a fire under his tail. It was the added motivation he needed to track down the trio of thieves/arsonists/stupid salamanders and put the bastards away.

"Shame we had to catch them all over again today," Kill scoffed. *"I still want to know how those assholes got out of that cell. Dusty had just reinforced the bars with that adjunct professor's newly formulated impenetrable, silver-plated, steel-reinforced paint. Not only should they not have been able to bend those bars, but the silver should have burned the skin off their bones. None of this shit is addin' up, boy-o."*

"We'll figure it out," Matt reassured, taking a deep breath in preparation to make an admission that might just make his head explode. *"Then, and only because you're right, I'll do as you say."*

"Well, shit," the Dragon King barked with laughter. *"That had to hurt. Sure you're not gonna spontaneously combust and kill us both? Go on, make my day. Tell me what I'm right about. It happens so often I can't keep up, and ya know how much I love hearing you admit it."*

"You, King Cillian of the Cumhachdach Red Dragon Clan, are absolutely and unequivocally correct. I should, and I will, make my mating to Dr. Delilah F. Weathersbee-Soon-to-be-Firestone official. I will have a proper Dragon Guard ceremony in the style of our ancestors and mark her with the power and magic of the Universe."

"And I thought you couldn't teach an old Guardsman new tricks."

"Just shut up and gloat quietly. I gotta—"

"Matt."

The chuckling in J.D.'s voice and the quick, sharp

snap of the Guardsman's fingers right beside his ear pulled Matt out of his revelry. "Yep, I'm here."

"Yeah, right, sure you are." Buck chuckled. "I've seen that look before. You were thinkin' 'bout a certain doctor with red hair and green eyes who just happens to be my mate's BFF."

"Yeah, well…"

"Yeah, well, focus on the food." J.D. chuckled. "Or Chase is gonna have it all eaten before we get so much as a crumb."

"Oh, hell, no, you don't," Matt teased, taking the honey roll the grizzly had just grabbed out of his big, meaty paw. "I'm hungry enough to eat my half and then some."

"Half?" J.D quickly objected. "No way, dude. We're all gettin' in on this action. No way we're lettin' you—"

"Get one freakin' bite of that grub before me," a loud voice jokingly threatened from across the room. Entering the diner, the heels of Ranger Evans' boots beat a staccato rhythm across the black and white tiles of the diner floor. The Special Agent with the Dragon Intelligence Agency and adopted MacAllen Dragon could barely contain his laughter as he added, "Y'all just left my ass out there in the desert with two of the nasty-ass, fuckin' St. Honoré brothers waitin' for FUC transport like I was the redheaded stepbrother."

Flopping down in the chair next to Matt, the DIA agent took off his dark brown Stetson and hit the professor in the back of the head, creating a cloud of dust. "And that's your job, Carrottop. How could you just leave me out there with treacherous, thieving fire salamander shifters waiting for *your* people? *Your* agents. *FUC* people. I'm DIA, not FUC. Hell, I just came to help as a favor. Thought you needed somebody to corral the troops, and I ended up doing all the heavy liftin'."

"Don't get it twisted, Range. You came because I called." Matt tried not to laugh at the scowl on the face of his longtime friend. "Because you lubs me. Because—"

"Oh, my Goddess, ditch the baby talk and save it for the doc. I should've just sent your ass to voicemail. Hit the little red button on that blasted phone, cuddled back up with Ellie, and had a blissful afternoon."

Laughing so hard he had to gasp to get the words out, Matt forced himself to speak, just to continue ribbing his brother from another mother. "Come on, Ranger, admit it. You can't resist a good chase. You're the big bad Special Agent who always gets his man. Nobody better to keep the St. Honoré brothers locked down tight till transport could get there. We knew you'd be okay. Besides, I had to contact the prisoners' sister and tell her to be on the lookout for the one that got away. I'm bettin' those boys will be out for blood, especially since she's the one who gave us their location in the first place."

"No way. That crap's not even close to my reason for haulin' ass," Chase corrected around a mouth full of food with a fresh honey roll in one hand and a piece of honey pecan pie in the other. "All I had to hear was 'homemade grub,' and I was outta there like a vampire in a silver mine. It'd been nearly three hours since my last meal. I was gettin' weak." Shoving the entire roll into his mouth, the grizzly kept right on talking. "Come on, you can't blame me. This is Sam's Diner, and they" —he lifted the index finger of his left hand while reaching for another roll—"are the Sampson twins. No way I was missin' out on this feast. Not even if my ass was on fire, man. This is the best I've had since the last time I was home."

"I hear ya, bud," Buck agreed, already filling his plate for the second time. "My stomach thought I'd cut my own thr—"

"What the fuck?!" Matt's roar cut off whatever the honey badger was about to say as the sound of hell breaking loose erupted just over their heads.

With windows shaking and the wooden chandeliers hanging from the ceiling swinging back and forth like a tornado was barreling through the place, a low, musical hum not unlike the trill of a hundred or so violins filled the air. Plates danced across the table, and food went flying in every direction. Glasses toppled and crashed, shattering into millions of pieces as water and sweet iced tea doused not only the food but the men at the table.

Then came an unholy roar, stabbing at Matt's eardrums like ice picks dipped in silver, making the hair covering his arms and at the nape of his neck stand on end. Jumping out of his chair and racing to the window, sure it was the Second Coming or, at the very least, one hell of a twister, the red dragon threw back the curtains just as Buck appeared at his side.

"Son of a bitch," the honey badger swore before Matt could take in the sight before him. "I'd know that jet stream anywhere." Looking over his shoulder, Buck added with a grin, "Hold on to your hats, boys. The Ladies of Disaster are about to land."

Chapter 3

"Left! Left! Hard left!" Del screamed, feet pounding on the pretend floor like she was driving Matilda and punching the brake to make the bright red Mini Cooper come to a screeching halt. Shame she was the passenger in the fastest jet the world had ever seen—without a clue how to fly the damned thing. "Hard left, Freddie! You're gonna—"

"I can see! I can see! Calm down, Del. Stop screaming. Do you honestly think the fact that we were thrown off course by a huge, freaky cloud of ash and smoke with eyes, a mouth, and claws and are now we're about to headbutt a mountain range has escaped my notice?"

"No," Del snapped. "I do not. I was trying to help. Trying to keep my head on my shoulders and my arms and legs in their anatomically correct positions. Excuse me for freaking out." Pushing out an exasperated breath, she worked hard to sound less like a lunatic and more like the highly acclaimed physician with ten degrees. "You know it's nuthin' personal. I trust you with my life and then some, but I have serious control issues. Nobody knows that better than you. I love you to bits. Nothing will ever change that, but I want to get my hands on that wheely thing worse than I wanna eat chocolate-covered cherries in bed with Matt. I. Need. To. Be. In. Control. That's no secret. It's just… It's just… Well, not being the one wearing the wings is hard for my crazy ass to handle. Ya know how much I like to be in the driver's seat. It's a character flaw I simply refuse to give up. It's my thing. It's who I am. Ya know what I'm sayin'?"

"Yeah, girl, I do, and don't ever change," Freddie grumbled through gritted teeth with half of a very forced smile making her look more than a little scary as she tried to keep the Lightfoot-Blackthorne FUC-U 2.0 from ending its maiden voyage as a pile of burning rubble.

Deciding it was better to shut her mouth and let her best friend keep them in the air, Del white-knuckled the harness strapped across her chest and refused to let her eyes slam shut. If she was going to die, then the strong, usually fearless dragonfly doctor was damned sure going to see it coming.

Then it happened—the call she'd been dreading. The one and only voice she'd hope to be back at FUCN'A before she heard it again. Right in the middle of her first-ever life-or-death situation, as she was sneaking off to parts unknown without telling another living soul—besides her bestie, who was piloting the plane—Matt psychically called.

"Del, my love." His voice floated through her mind. Using their unique telepathy, one of the many magical benefits some mates were blessed with, he whispered, *"Was that you and Freddie who just divebombed Sam's Diner in Valentine, Texas?"*

Busted! How could she have forgotten that her dragon, along with Chase Brownsmith and Buck—Freddie's mate—were less than a hundred miles from the exact spot she and the winged tree frog had unearthed the precious pahoehoe crystals? The very place they were heading to at that very moment.

Maybe everything would be okay. Maybe Del could bluff her way out of it. Not lie, no, she would never lie to her mate—or anyone else for that matter. However, she would admit to forgetting to give him a heads-up and say she was sorry at least a hundred times, maybe even cook his favorite meal and come to the table in that slinky little black dress Matt loved so much.

"Damned straight, sista," Suri sassed, her tone as sharp as ever while all four of her gorgeous, glittery, mosaic blue and green wings fluttered in double time in Del's mind's eye. *"You will not leave us single and raising a bunch of cats in a shack on the dragonfly side of the Swamp. Not that there's anything wrong with being a dragonfly cat lady. I mean, it's what some people aspire to. I'm sure there are even some guys who think it's fun. Of course, they'd be dragonfly cat dudes, and for the record, I find all of it kinda noble. If they have no mate, or theirs left*

this mortal plane way too early, then who am I to criticize a person's life choices? After all, cats need love, too. Remember that tabby cat shifter we met in Iowa? What was his name?"

"Felix."

"Yeah, him. Can you believe his mom named him Felix? What was she thinking? I mean—"

"Can you get on with my scolding? I'm about to die here, and I would like to do it with a little peace and quiet."

"Oh hell no! We are not gonna die, and while I'm at it, you, Delilah Flashwing Weathersbee-Soon-to-be-Firestone, the dragonfly cat lady gig is in no way, shape, or form our situation, and you know it. We have a mate—one heck of an amazing mate. And you will not now or ever lie to that hunka-hunka-dragon-hotness. And while I'm at it, the only reason we are still single is because you—"

"Okay, okay, chill with the riot act. I get it. You know I didn't dare go there. Good Goddess in a G-string, Suri, we share a brain. You absolutely, without a single doubt, heard what I was thinking. I never came within a hundred miles of entertaining the thought of being like—"

"Do not even say that silly woman's name," Princess of the Blue Empress Dragonflies of South America hissed. *"I just can't take it. We tried until we were blue in the face to tell her to be careful, stay away from the ambrosia punch. I even told the whole sordid story of my own sister, Sakayama —a cautionary tale about partying with the fairies—but nothing worked."*

Unfortunately, Suri was right—as usual. Draya didn't listen to Del's sisterly advice. She completely ignored the guidance of her own dragonfly. Worst of all, she totally dismissed the oldest, wisest, and most tenacious quad-winged shifter in all the world, their great-granny Em—who happened to have said that Devin wasn't the right lizard for her oldest granddaughter in the first place. Nope, Granny never was one for what she called "cross mating" unless she felt the "spirit of the Universe in the tips of her wings."

Thank the Great Goddess, not only had Em's wings tingled, but the very day Del met Matt, the matriarch had a dream confirming the couple's mating. There was no doubt in the doc's mind that Granny was going to love her mate. He was the elderly dragonfly's kind of dragon.

Shame Draya hadn't had the same luck…

"Could the wise, old Queen have been right?" Del questioned before quickly adding, *"Do not answer that, Suri. Just save the speech for another day."*

However, since she'd thought about it, Del was forced to let the whole sad story run its course in her brain. It was so pitiful. Yes, it was Draya's own fault, but Del still felt terrible. How could she not? They were sisters. She only wished she could've helped.

It didn't matter that Draya had ignored all her counsel. If only Del could've been there to give her oldest sister a hug and hold her hand as a shitstorm of mountainous proportions exploded in her face.

It was all so stupid and completely avoidable. Why hadn't the eldest daughter of the king and queen of the Blue Empress Dragonfly Shifters just listened to everyone's advice or, at the very least, not gotten shit-faced drunk on the headiest drink ever created, fairy ambrosia? Was it really too much to ask? It must have been because, after four shots and an ambrosia cosmo, Draya right and truly snogged a fairy stripper then groped his sexy bum right in the middle of the dance floor.

At her own bachelorette party...

Where all her friends and *their cellphones* were in attendance...

Yes, she'd always been a party girl. Sure, she was the one sister out of seven most likely to dance on table-tops, but the undeniable fact was that *she knew better*. Not only was she the utmost social media influencer, but she'd made the same status possible for every one of her over-indulged, super-spoiled entourage. They'd been snapping pics and posting the scoop for almost a decade. Draya's Devilish Deeds had nearly five million followers. What happened next shouldn't have surprised anyone.

When the incriminating photos hit HocusPocus-Hotspot—the supernatural social media "place to be" on Ghougle, the paranormal dark web created and maintained by Nostradamus and his kickass girlfriend, Emily—the very next morning, well, the shit well and truly hit the fan. Draya's mate didn't even bother breaking up with her in person. The rat bastard—make that grungy, greedy, gag-worthy gecko—commented under the said pictures by saying, *Have a nice life. Lose my number.*

The fallout had been heinous. People pointed and

laughed everywhere she went. Draya was still in hiding. And Granny Em was calling in favors from every supe she'd ever known to have a particular gecko named Devin turned into a grub worm and eaten by the stinkiest armadillo shifter she could locate.

But none of that mattered at the moment. Del's memories only served as a reminder to always do the right thing. She needed to deal with her own mate, the one she would spend the rest of forever with, and she needed to do it fast. Matt was one smart cookie. He never asked a question he didn't already have the answer to. Her man was not only good-looking, but he was smart as a whip. A lethal combination that made Del weak in the knees.

"No way! No way! No way!" she screamed. "This cannot be happening!"

"And it's not," Freddie snapped in response. "Nothing's gonna happen. No way. No how. I'm the best-damned pilot this world's ever—"

"Not that!" Del yelled, jabbing the tip of her index finger against her temple as she leaned toward her bestie. "Matt! Matthew! Professor Matthew Firestone. My man. My mate. My dragon. My—"

"I know who your mate is, Del. Duh. I knew him first. Was there when you met him. Am gonna be your matron of honor. Getta grip! I haven't lost my memory, and I'm damned sure not losing my plane or my best friend."

"Getta grip? Getta grip? Did you seriously just tell

me to getta—ahhhhhhhh… shit shit shit shit shit shit shiiiiiiiiitttttt! Watch out!"

And thank the Great Goddess, Freddie did just that as she yanked the leopard print, pleather-covered yoke of the FUC-U 2.0 back as hard and fast as she could. Watching in utter amazement as the nose of the jet popped up toward the sky, Del's head whipped to the side, and she gasped, "Oh, my Goddess, you are amazing! Are you okay? Can you breathe? Are you breathing? What can I—"

"N-Nothing." Freddie croaked the answer to the question Del hadn't been able to complete. Continuing to take in the totally fantastic way her best friend straddled the yoke of her highly prized, newly finished, and heavily modified Lightfoot-Blackthorne FUC-U 2.0, the dragonfly doc gave a wide-eyed stare as her mouth hung open.

Steering with not only her hands but apparently her incredibly toned gluteus maximus, if Del knew her anatomy—which she most assuredly did—Freddie snarled through tightly gritted teeth, "Put your head between your legs and kiss your ass hello, 'cause this landing's gonna be one for the books. Hell, I might even write a paper about it. Use that shit to teach others. Make sure all the FUC pilots know how to pull this off. Ya never know when it might come in handy. We'll call it the Freddie Flip and Flow."

Del's adrenaline kicked into an even higher gear, ready for every second of the action. Her heart pounded hard, close to how it had when she performed surgery on all three hearts of an octopus on a coral reef off the coast of Florida—really, really close.

Making a mental note, Del promised herself to have Freddie and Dusty teach her to fly a plane as soon as dragonflyily possible. Whipping through the air with Suri's wings was nothing short of amazing, but the power of having control over tons of metal, fiberglass, kryptonite fiber-gloopolymer composite, and blazing engines would be the next level and then some.

Holding on to the harness, the doc's boobs mashed flat to her chest as she opened her eyes even wider and whooped, "Yeehaw!"

It was great! However, there was a bigger, possibly catastrophic, problem that had nothing to do with flying. Del—one of the most brilliant women, shifters, and doctors in the world—had forgotten to lock her mental shields back into place after getting Matt's initial contact. Hence, and absolutely unfortunately, the next thing she heard, in living, breathing Dolby stereo from the inside and outside of her head, was, *"What the fuck are you yee hawing about? This is not the time to be throwin' a party!"*

Opening her mouth to answer Freddie—not her mate, because she hadn't come up with what she was going to say—at the precise moment that the nose of the Lightfoot-Blackthorne FUC-U 2.0 straightened out, Del instead was once again screaming, "Watch out!"

And with her shields still wide open and broadcasting loud and clear, her mate also heard the rather frantic and absolutely freaked-out declaration. Which led to her alter-ego's sarcastic, *"Way to go, Del. Way. To. Go."*

Unable to formulate even the slightest of snappy comebacks to Suri's unsolicited rebuke, the doc's eyes were glued to the prickly tops of giant cacti, the pointy tips of massive mesas, and more than ten pillows full of feathers from the asses of a flock of red-shouldered hawks being severed from their rightful places by the nose, engines, and tailwind of Freddie's jet. There was no denying that her heart was in her throat, and visions of becoming one or more of the floating feathers entered her mind. It even made her wonder if her number might really be up.

Leaning forward as far as the harness across her chest would allow, she plastered her face against the windshield and looked straight down to the sandy earth below. "Aren't we supposed to be—"

"Don't you worry that pretty red head of yours," Freddie ordered. "Sit back, hold on, and don't even think about puking on the upholstery. That stench will blow the new jet smell all to hell."

Doing as she was told without hesitation, reservation, or a whisper of a thought, all Del could do was inhale sharply and trust her bestie. Getting as far as turning her head to the side, she smiled from ear-to-ear when Freddie hopped off the yoke, put her hands right back where they'd been a second before, shoved the damned thing forward as far as it would go, and cheered, "Hell yeah, I love it when a plan comes together."

Dumbfounded, unable to think, to speak, to even so much as breathe, Del watched in awe as the winged tree frog's hands, feet, and mouth moved so quickly they were nothing but a blur. Whether Freddie was talking to Del, FUC-U 2.0, or the Great Goddess herself, the doc had no idea, nor the time to ask.

Jerking the yoke one way then the other, her feet working pedals the doc hadn't known were there until that very moment, Freddie was moving faster than Del had ever seen. The doc could *not* believe her eyes, nor could she understand one damned, rambled, smooshed-together word Freddie was saying, but that didn't matter. She trusted her friend's ability, and seeing the winged tree frog in action was not only breathtaking but reaffirmed Del's belief in her friend a hundred times over.

"And down we go!"

"Hell yeah," Del whooped. "Let's do this thing!"

Eyes front, smiling so wide her pearly whites were shining in the rays of the setting sun, the dragonfly doctor instinctually knew the exact bull's-eye of her friend's aim. It was high. It was flat. It was wide. It was the only rock-topped mountain in sight. And it was so close Del could count the cracks.

One quick circle around the peak, another forward shove of the yoke, and just like that, the Lightfoot-Blackthorne FUC-U 2.0 was headed in for a perfect landing. Hitting the ground with the tiniest of bumps, the jet was still in one piece as Del watched Freddie pull back the yoke, hit buttons like she was frantically dialing an overseas number, then sit back in her seat and smile proudly.

"Wow! Is that what you call a good landing?" Del chuckled, brushing the long strands of red hair that had escaped her ponytail out of her eyes before unbuckling her harness.

"No, girl." Freddie snickered, her head falling to the side, her grin growing to a full-blown smile. "A *good* landing is one you can walk away from. A *great* landing, like the one yours truly just executed, is one where you can use the plane again."

Laughing out loud, Del made it as far as, "Well, if we'd have stopped to get that tequila before blasting off, I'd make some magnanimous toast about the wonders of your greatness. But—"

And that was when Matt's roar shook the confines of her brain.

"Delilah Weathersbee-Soon-to-be-Firestone, you better answer me right this minute. Just tell me you're okay. Hell, tell me anything. I'm freaking the hell out. Seriously, losing my shit. Ready to lose my mind and go all scaly. Maybe grow some wings. Let Kill outta the bag. I love you, Del. Love you more than anything. I've never manhandled you or gone all alpha-dragon. Goddess knows I can control myself, but let me tell you, it's not a pretty sight. Okay, it's a little pretty. The old man's got some gorgeous ruby scales, but... but... but that's not the point, is it? No, it is not. I'm not above losing all semblance of cool and calm when I'm scared

and trying to keep you safe. Well, not the manhandling. That's just bullshit. I'd never do that. You know that, right? But never doubt the fact that I'd add an extra dose of alpha-dragon and a couple shit-ton of Neanderthal just to keep you out of harm's way. I swear to all that's holy, I'll scoop you up, throw you over my shoulder, and smack that gorgeous ass of yours."

A deep inhale—one she could only imagine was accompanied by the irresistibly handsome flush of his face and flames dancing in his beautiful blue eyes—was the only break Matt took. Sadly, it wasn't long enough for Del to shove a word in edgewise before her mate was right back at it.

"I'll do it, Delly Bell. I'll do it, and I won't even care how mad you are at me. I'll carry you all the way back to our home in Nonamesville, British Columbia, chain you to our bed without a stitch of clothing, and never let you out of my sight again. Don't tempt me, Del. You know I can do it."

"Oh, shit, Matt," she gasped. *"I'm so sorry. I didn't... I mean, we were... Well, it's a long... That is to say...* arrrrgggghhhhh!*"*

With no warning—not even the tiniest groan of the super-secret, highly classified, and, to anyone who asked, totally nonexistent kryptonite fiber-gloopolymer composite she'd invented especially for Freddie's new improved Lightfoot-Blackthorne FUC-U 2.0—Del, her dearest friend, and said aircraft were plummeting straight to hell at a high rate of speed. Layer after layer of soil crusts, every make, model, and description she'd read about, learned of, or imagined in her wildest dreams, flew by like the colors, shapes, and lights of a kaleidoscope on a sugar high.

Screaming at the top of her lungs, with Freddie doing the same right beside her, Del tried with all her might to calm down. Flipping through the imaginary Rolodex in her brain, the one where she kept all her best ideas and theories, the doc attempted to think of a way to stop their downward plunge. She inhaled and exhaled. She counted to three. She even pictured her happy place—in Matt's arms after a night of lovemaking.

But still, there was nothing.

Magic flew inside, outside, and all around the jet. Swirls and rainbows, flashes and bolts—every color of red, orange, yellow, green, indigo, and blue—intertwining, overlapping, and twisting in on each other. It was a festival of fireworks created by two immensely magical women and the alter egos with whom they shared their souls.

But it was no use. It was as if the universe, fate, and destiny had put a plan in place that no one but the Almighty Three could stop, and those crazy assholes were nowhere to be found.

The thought of going splat, of being a greasy spot at the bottom of a deep dark hole in the middle of the desert, was playing on a continuous, unending loop in Del's brain. Suri was screaming, *"More! More! Give it all you got! Grab the magic from the center of the earth. Mother Nature damned sure owes us one from the time we stopped Old Faithful from killing President Roosevelt. We gotta get back to that hot-ass dragon. I'm too young to die! The world needs me!"*

Falling for what seemed like forever—but actually couldn't have been longer than a couple of seconds—the dragonfly doctor, her best friend, and the highly modified, one-of-a-kind jet came to a screeching stop. There was no crashing or bloodshed. Not even a scratch. They just halted as quickly as they'd started falling, and at precisely the same time that Del screamed, "I can't die before I'm married!"

"And you won't, dingleberry!"

Holding her breath to the count of three, afraid to so much as let her eyes slide to the side, Del barked with laughter when Freddie added, with a growl, "And in case I hadn't mentioned this, I effin' hate it when a perfectly executed plan goes straight to hell in an effed-up handbasket. Somebody call the Almighty Three and lodge a complaint. I want compensation, and I want it now."

Chapter 4

"Del. Del? Delilah!"

Bellowing through their mating bond, that beautiful glowing strand of miraculous magic connecting his mind to his dragonfly's, Matt spun on the heels of his boots at the same time that Buck tapped on his shoulder.

"What the fuck do you want?" he roared. His mind and heart raced from the possibility of something horrible and terrible happening to his mate, and his hard-fought control unraveled at the seams.

Hands in the air, the honey badger chuckled his mock surrender. "Whoa, dude, hold your fire. I come in peace."

"Oh, shit! Sorry," Matt rushed out, embarrassment at his outburst adding to his already raging emotions. "I'm freakin' the fuck out. Can't get a hold of Del. I was talkin' to her then…."

"Nothing?" Buck finished. "I know. Me, too."

Tapping his temple, he continued. "It's radio silence. One minute Freddie was there, and then *zip, zing, blammo,* she was gone. Not even a peep out of her crazy winged tree frog, Rainbow Bright."

"Oh, shit," Matt spat, immediately mentally barking at his Dragon King. *"Have you tried Del or Suri? I can't—"*

"No, really? You can't get a hold of Del?" Kill deadpanned, his sarcasm so thick Matt could've cut it with a butter knife. *"Color me surprised. It's not like you were just telepathically screaming like a banshee in the middle of a battlefield at our sweet, little dragonfly. Hell, you've been quiet as a church mouse all day long. I was just sittin' here, enjoying the quiet, wondering what you were up to, polishin' my scales. Not givin' a diddly damn that you might very well have deafened me for life."*

A split-second pause, one filled with rage, anger, and more than a bit of irritation, and the Dragon King snarled, *"Are you barkin' mad? You're blowing the little gray cells right outta my skull. I would have to be deaf not to know Del was in trouble and dumb as a post not to have already tried to reach both her and Suri. Of course, I've called to our perfect mate and her sassy alter-ego. I was on it before the thought made it across your thick skull. And before you ask, I can't reach either one of them."*

"But..."

"But you didn't hear me? Could it be because you're using enough magic to have every corpse between Valentine and Juarez climbin' outta the ground and hot-footin' it to our mate? That the very universe Herself is wondering what the hell is wrong with you? That our ancestors are calling all

the way from the Isle of Skye wondering what the hell just happened? That?"

"Kiss my ass," the Guardsman snarled. *"I need to find—"*

"Del?" Kill scoffed. *"No shit, Sherlock. Let's get the hell outta Dodge. This is gonna be a boots-on-the-ground mission. Heaven knows you've already wasted enough bloody time making my ears bleed and givin' me a migraine."*

Stepping around Buck as the Dragon King continued to give him hell, Matt raced across the diner, threw open the door, and called over his shoulder, "I'll call y'all when I get out there. Just be—"

"No," came an adamant and unison reply that had his head snapping to the side and the words freezing on his tongue.

Meeting the eyes of some of the best men and two of the sassiest she-wolves Matt had ever known, pride and emotion filled his every fiber. "Y'all don't have to—"

"Yeah, right," Buck harrumphed. "Like I'm gonna stay here while you go runnin' off to save our mates. First of all, ain't no fuckin' way. Second of all, I need Freddie more than I need air, and thirdly—"

"He'd never hear the end of it," Chase chuckled, his larger-than-life confidence just what Matt needed to calm his frayed nerves and get him thinking straight. "That winged tree frog of his would jerk a knot in his tail the size of Texas if old Buck here wasn't right by your side."

"Damned straight. Now—"

"Now shut the hell up," Chase growled. "I've given y'all my best rah-rah speech, and that's all you're gettin'. Let's get goin'. The sooner we grab your mates, the quicker I can get back here and have a couple more pieces of that awesome honey pecan pie."

Out the door and three steps into the parking lot was as long as Matt could wait. From one beat of his heart to the next, the enchantment of the Ancients filled his body. Bright red scales hovered over his entire body, bones elongated, muscles ripped and tore, and then, in the blink of an eye, his massive wings unfurled in the last blasting rays of the setting sun.

Shifting into his dragon was nothing short of invigorating. It was who and what he was meant to be. Kill was the embodiment of fierce power, loyal determination, and the unending need to be certain good always prevailed.

Leaving J.D., Mason, and Ranger to play dragon taxi for their friends without wings, Kill's massive back paws raced across the parking lot while Matt called to his mate for the hundredth time. With a single backward thrust of his wings, the feeling of pure, white dragon magic filling every fiber of their combined being, and just like that, the giant red dragon took to the skies as if he were shot out of a cannon. Following the glittering trail only he and Kill could see, the connection they shared with Del and Suri, Guardsman and dragon made a beeline for their dragonfly.

"I thought you said the ladies were working on a formula to return Dino Dave back to Alexander," Kill grumped.

"That usually means they're blowing up something. How the hell did they end up out here?"

"I have no idea," came Matt's sharp retort. *"Haven't talked to Del since early this morning. We were still in bed when I got the call that the St. Honoré brothers had escaped. Got dressed, kissed her goodbye, and hauled ass out here. Furthermore, you know all that because, as you said, you're with me all the time, so this next part will be no surprise."*

"Yeah, yeah, yeah," Kill huffed. "Let me finish that thought for ya. We—"

"Oh, hell no," Matt jumped in. "I get to finish this one. It's so rare that I get to be right. I'm gonna enjoy saying I was right here with you when they damned near took the roof off Sam's Diner. Have been with you all day, just like every day, so you know that I haven't talked to Del and have not the foggiest idea in the whole damned world what she and Freddie are doing out here."

"Okay, okay," Kill huffed. *"No need to get any pissier than you normally are. I just thought maybe you had a clue. A guess. Goddess knows you and Del have split your time between helping Dr. Anatoli and makin' sweet, sweet love—"*

"What did I tell you about my love life?"

"Something stupid, like it was off-limits," Kill scoffed. *"As if. You do remember that we share a brain, right? That we're connected at the little gray cells like wallpaper and paste. That even if I have my headphones on and happen to be watching my shows, I still know what's going on, right? That I'm right there with you every minute of every day, whether I want to be or not. So, when I say that you are over the moon, ga-ga, crazy in love with that cute little dragonfly"*

—*a* sharp inhale, a flutter of his huge eyelids, which literally cut off all light from the outside world for a split second, and the Dragon King kept going—*"and I couldn't be happier for us. Just fess up, tell me I'm right, and things will go a lot smoother."*

"But I have fessed up. Did you already forget? Yeah, you're old, but—"

"Hey there, young'un, not cool bringin' up my age. To be honest, it's just rude. I remember exactly what you said, but again I ask, why are we not officially mated to that red-haired goddess with sparkling emerald eyes and a smile that knocks my socks off?"

"You don't wear socks."

"Ha, ha, ha," Kill mocked. *"Lookie there, folks. Matt Firestone finally got a sense of humor."*

"I hate you."

"No, you don't." Kill laughed out loud, the deep rumble forcing Matt to grin right along.

"Pay attention," the Guardsman barked, his focus instantly intense and unwavering as the connection he shared with Del flashed brighter.

Looking through the Dragon King's eyes was always amazing, no matter how many times he did it. Not only did he get a three-hundred-and-forty-degree field of vision because of their position on either side of Kill's massive noggin, but with those huge golden orbs and their elliptical pupils, it seemed as if Matt could see forever. However, he still couldn't catch a glimpse of Del or Freddie or the jet on this occasion.

"She has to be here. Can't you feel it? She's close."

"Never fear." Kill's deep rumble invaded his thoughts. *"They're inside that pile of rocks straight ahead."*

Following the invisible line extending from the farthest tip of Kill's outstretched wing, Matt growled through gritted teeth, *"Had to be Devil's Peak. Why did it have to be Devil's Peak? Have I mentioned how very much I hate Devil's Peak?"*

"A time or two," the Dragon King sighed. *"But maybe you can tell me again and be sure to say the name four or five more times. I might forget it in my old age."*

"I really do hate you."

"You really don't," Kill snickered. *"Now, to answer your question, our one-and-only amazing dragonfly is inside Devil's Peak because the Universe doesn't give us any more than we can handle, and you, my friend, are one tough son of a gun."*

"Okay, Confucius," Matt scoffed. *"Maybe you can enlighten me later about the wonders of the Universe. I must've missed that in Philosophy 101."*

"Count on it."

Not taking the bait or the chance of winding up in another battle of wits with one of the most formidable mental strategists the world had ever known, Matt let Kill steer the dragon as they got closer to the highest summit in the Chihuahua Desert.

Moving to the rear of their shared consciousness, the Guardsman tried again to reach his mate. With all the hope and faith he had in the Almighty Three—knowing they would keep Del safe—filling his heart, the Guardsman let his eyes slide shut and pictured her beautiful face.

Adding in some Gaelic, the language of the Ancients, what Del called their very own language of love, Matt breathed, *"Delilah,* mo chroí, m 'ionmhas, fìor bhuille mo chridhe, *is everything okay? Can I—"*

"Oh, for Pete's sake, Del," Kill added. *"Matt's lost his ever-lovin' mind. Not knowing where you are has short-circuited his brain, wiped away all his good sense, and reduced your boy here to a mumbling mess of... of... well, hell, Del, he's just a damned mess. Can you please give us a little flash of your sexy magic, or a smoke signal, or a...what the fuck is that?"*

Holding on for dear life as Kill barrel-rolled to the left, jerked to a stop, and rolled in the opposite direction, the Guardsman almost lost his lunch. Then the Dragon King pulled his wings tight to his side and pointed the tip of his snout at the side of the red clay mountain, and Matt screamed, *"Is that a... That can't be a... No, it's a..."*

"Yes, genius," Kill snarled through gritted teeth. *"It's a huge, freaky cloud of ash and smoke with glowing red eyes, a mouth full of fangs, and claws damned near as big as mine, but you wanna know what the worst part is?"*

"What?! What could possibly be worse? Son of a bitch!"

"Yep, you guessed it," Kill sarcastically grimaced. *"Being swallowed by the same monstrous cloud, being forced to watch the whole damned thing, and not being able to do one damned thing about it."*

"Well, shit," Matt groaned. *"Guess Chase gets to eat my piece of pie."*

"Oh, buddy, it's better than th—"

An evil cackle, like nails on a chalkboard, or sandpaper on steel, cut off what Kill was saying, attacking their combined consciousness with treacherous shards of ice.

"Wh-What...the f-fuck...is up-up w-with the ar-arctic winds?" Matt stammered and stuttered.

"Hell, if I know," Kill snapped. *"It's takin' everything I got to keep us from turning into a dragon Popsicle."*

"Damn it a-all to h-hell, I h-hate the c-c-cold!"

Landing with a bone-jarring thud, Matt's head connected with a massive block of frozen earth, prickly from a massive amount of sand, with such force that he wondered if there were stars and tweety birds dancing around his head. Then Kill groaned, *"Damn, son, this is the worse hangover I've ever had,"* and the Guardsman knew he was in trouble.

Forcing the shift as his Dragon King passed out, Matt jumped to his feet, grabbed the wall to stay upright, and threw his preternatural senses as far and wide as they would go. Holding his forehead with his free hand, he mumbled under his breath, "Kill was right. I need three bottles of ibuprofen, five pounds of ice, and three days in bed—with Del." Shivering despite his efforts to the contrary, he added with a growl, "And a heating pad and electric blanket."

Turning left and right and left again, he spun in

circles one way then the other, all the way round at least twice and then some. More frustrated than he could ever remember being, when not even his enhanced vision plus the magic he was siphoning from Kill failed to cut through the frigid darkness, he growled, "What the fuck is goin' on? How the…*ahhhhhhhhh*!!"

Once again thrown through the pitch-black darkness, screaming his fool head off with hands and feet flailing about like he was a turtle stuck on his back, Matt's fingers reached as far as they could, trying to grab anything that might be sticking out of the walls. Head crashing into another wall of rock or ice or frozen sand or whatever the hell was inside a volcano in the middle of the desert, the Guardsman slid down the wall like ice cream melting all over a little kid's hand.

"Ugh!" Whatever air was left in his lungs came rushing out as his stomach made contact with a very hard, extremely pointed pile of something he truly didn't want to identify.

Flopping like a fish out of water, Matt had just gotten his first inhale of wonderfully fresh air when stinky, nasty black magic came out of nowhere, zipping and zapping in every direction. Rolling one way then the other, getting on his knees only to be knocked down, he stuck his butt in the air then slammed his stomach to the floor.

"Well, shit, this might just work." Repeating the action over and over, giving whoever was trying to turn him into a burnt French fry the show of a lifetime

—a Guardsman imitating an inch worm—his gaze flew as far as they would go in every direction trying to get a bead on the asshole.

"I know you're there!" He roared. "I'm not doing' this shit to myself!" Repeating the inchworm movement. Matt spat, "Fucking dick knows he's got me cornered. Have I mentioned how much I hate being blind, scorched, and lying around like a sitting duck in enemy territory?"

Waiting for a snappy comeback from Kill, disappointed when he remembered the Dragon King was down for the count, he snarled, "Well, I did, and I do, dammit."

Up, down, up, down, humping his way across the craggiest surface in the world, Matt was just about to snarl at his Dragon King one more time when, for the third damned time, the crown of his head rammed into an impenetrable, cold-as-hell embankment. "Son of a bitch!" he spat. "This shit is...*ahhhhhh*!"

Whipping his head forward, fighting against the fiery talons ripping through his scalp, fisting his hair, and trying to pull his head off his shoulders, he got as far as, "Let me go, you stupid mother fuc—" before his neck was jerked backward and the snout of the ugliest, nastiest, biggest amphibian he'd ever seen was shoved into his face.

"Why couldn't you just leave well enough alone? What the hell is your problem? Why do you FUC dicks just keep comin'?"

Swimming between consciousness and unconsciousness, head pounding like a jackhammer beating away at concrete, and his neck resembling a pool noodle after a long hard summer, Matt searched his poor muddled brain to place that voice. He'd heard it before. Hell, he'd been threatened by the same stupid, slurring lisp so many times they were all running together in his mind.

"Who the fu—"

"Shut the hell up!" his captor roared, slamming Matt's head against an incredibly hard surface—a scorching hot and stinking-of-sulfur surface. "I swear to the Goddess, I'm gonna beat you black and blue, Matt Firestone, but first, imma gonna rip the wings off that little dragonfly of yours."

Chapter 5

“Okay, I give.” Freddie shrugged. “Where the hell are we?”

“Would you believe inside a volcano in the middle of the Chihuahua Desert?” Del replied.

"Well, duh. I was there for that, remember? At least you didn't say, Have you heard the one about the winged tree frog and the dragonfly and a plane ride gone wrong?" Freddie sarcastically snickered. "'Cause then I might've bopped you in the head."

"Hey, now," Del huffed, trying to act affronted but failing miserably and unable to stop grinning no matter how hard she tried. "No bopping." Laughing out loud despite the situation, she went on. "I've gotten bops in the head from you before, and that shit hurts. And that one time you left a mark."

"Yeah, still sorry about that. Sometimes Rainbow Bright forgets her own strength." Raising her eyebrows, batting her eyes, and tilting her head in the cutest way,

Del's bestie even pushed out her bottom lip and gave a cute little pout.

"Oh, come on, that's pouring it on a little thick, even for you."

“But it worked!” Freddie cheered, giving the doc a high-five.

"That it did." Del giggled then moved on to what she really wanted to know. "So, who is this living, breathing shifter you know who might be able to help us help Dusty and…" Taking a deep breath, she added, "Can she get this huge jet—plus us—outta this volcano?"

"Well, I'm sure she could, but—"

"There's a shroud of magic as thick as my thigh, as wide as the swamp, and stickier than the crap Nanny uses to glue fake nails to her fingertips all around this place." Del finished her best friend's thought.

Touching the tip of her nose with the end of her finger, then pointing at Del, Freddie made a clicking sound with her tongue against her teeth and confirmed, "You know it. So, here's what I'm thinkin'."

Unfortunately, Del never got to hear what her friend was going to say, as the popping and crackling of ice covering the outside of the kryptonite fiber-gloopolymer composite hull thundered inside the FUC-U 2.0. Spinning in her seat, palms slapping onto the window to her right, the doc shrieked, "What the hell? How is this happening? It's ice! Honest-to-the-Goddess sheets of freaking ice. It's coming out of nowhere, in the bottom of a freaking volcano in the middle of one of the hottest places on earth!"

Whirling back the other way, Del screeched, "Why aren't you—?" Slapping the pilot's seat like it was on fire, her eyes glued to her bestie's jug of coffee, she screamed at the top of her lungs, "Freddie! Freddie! Winifred Lightfoot-Blackthorne, where the hell are you?! I know you can't be far. Your coffee's still here!" Waiting the span of a single heartbeat, she added with a growl, "Come out, or I'll drink every frikkin' drop!"

Out of her seat and jumping to her feet, Del ran from the front of the jet to the back, opening compartments and cabinets and anything else she could get her hands on, screeching her bestie's name like a mantra to the gods.

Doing another lap inside, she stopped dead as Suri yelled, *"Will you please shut up? Freddie's not here. You can see she's not here. Screaming her name again and again and again isn't gonna make her be here. We've talked about this before. You cannot magick a person out of thin air by screaming like a banshee."*

"But—"

"But what? Did you suddenly become a sorceress?"

"No, but—"

"Are you Cinderella's fairy godmother? Should I expect you to float through the air singing bibbidi-bobbidi-boo and waving a magic wand?"

"No, it's just that—"

"That what, Del? That you're freaking the hell out and don't know what to do and would like a little help before

we're both curled up in the fetal position over in that corner singing 'The Itsy Bitsy Spider'?"

"Ummm, yeah, kinda."

"Well, good, at least we can agree about something."

Trying to speak, but not quick enough to squeeze a word in edgewise, the doc was forced to listen as her dragonfly alter-ego continued to rant. *"First things first, we need to get the heck away from this plane before it collapses in on itself. I have a—"*

"It won't do that."

"Won't do what? What? Won't. Do. What?"

"The plane won't collapse in on itself."

"Okay, look, I know I slept through most of those millions of hours of classes you insisted we attend. You know school is not my thing, and, well, it so very much your thing. So, although you think I wasn't listening, there were a few times that I was, and one of them just happened to be when that sexy-ass professor with the longish blond hair and dark brown eyes who used to—"

"Professor Whitman."

"Yeah, him. Anyway, when he used to talk about the force of matter and the weight of liquid water versus water vapor versus frozen water—"

"Ice."

"Yes, ice, dumbass," Suri growled, making Del smirk because, for one of the few times in all their years together, the doc was actually getting the upper hand. *"As I was saying—"*

"As you were saying, ice weighs more than water and vapor, and you are right. Also, in most cases, ice would

crunch a plane like an empty beer can. However, the FUC-U 2.0 is made with my super-secret and, to the rest of the world, non-existent kryptonite fiber-gloopolymer composite that—"

"Oh, wait, I remember this one." Suri whooped like she'd just won the lottery or met the dragonfly of her dreams—or both. *"That kryogenetic gloopity-glop—"*

"Kryptonite fiber-gloopolymer composite."

"Yeah, that crap you whipped up in the lab. It can withstand temperatures above 5000 degrees Fahrenheit, atmospheres more oppressive than the one on Venus, and a pressure that is equal to more pounds per square inch than an elephant standing on the head of a dressmaker's pin."

"Exactly!" It was Del's turn to whoop. It was fantastic that something—anything—had gotten into Suri's thick skull, and the doc wanted to congratulate her alter-ego. *"I am so proud of you. I can't believe you were—"*

"Okay, Billie Jo Nye, the wannabe science girl. I know this science stuff is important to you, but I couldn't give a diddly-doo-op. I just need to know what it means for me and how that saves my cute little booty from being smashed inside this tin can of an airplane."

"Have I mentioned lately how very much you infuriate me and how I wish the Great Goddess had a form I could fill out to get a new dragonfly alter-ego to live in my brain?"

"Yes, as many times as I've explained that you're stuck with me, and you're the lucky one. I am Princess Surama—"

"Blah, blah, blah, Princess of my ass," Del snarled. *"And to answer your question, there is no way you're gonna get*

smashed *in the Lightfoot-Blackthorne FUC-U 2.0 because it is made with the strongest stuff on the planet—probably any other planet, too, but I haven't been anywhere but this planet to test it yet. You're welcome very much. Furthermore, I am gonna tell Freddie that you called her jet—and I quote* —a tin can of an airplane—*unquote—just as soon as I find her."*

"No, please, Del, I can't—"

"Save it, dragonfly ass," the doc snapped, not sure if she was angrier at her alter-ego for being such an obstinate butthead or herself for giving in and arguing with her obstinate butthead of an alter-ego.

Either way, Del was so irritated and utterly frustrated that she hit the big red button, which opened the door and lowered the clamshell airstair, and threw her foot out into the open before looking to see that the coast was clear. No sooner had the soles of her favorite powder-blue Chuck Taylor Converse high tops hit the step than a stream of flames flew past her head.

"What the fu—"

"No, no, no, oh my golly, I'm so sorry, don't shoot," the softest, sweetest little voice she'd ever heard yelped.

"Don't shoot?" Del shrieked. "It's you that's shootin' fireballs. I'm the one up here bobbin' and weavin'."

"Oh my gosh, oh my gosh, oh my gosh, I didn't mean to do that. Please don't hate me, but your hair's on fire, and the crack closed."

"The *what* closed?" Del roared, slapping the side of her head like it was—well, like it was on fire, because it was. Cursing and cussing, she stumbled and skipped her way down the steps, just barely staying upright until she was on level ground and standing right in front of the cutest petite brunette with glowing golden eyes and an uneasy smile.

More irritated than she wanted to admit that she'd let her guard down and one of her curls was still smoldering, the doc barked, "Who the hell are you? What crack are you talking about? And..." Closing the distance between them and pointing her finger at the tip of the woman's nose, she snarled, "Where's my best friend? I swear to all that's holy if you've harmed a hair on her—"

"Whoa, whoa, whoa there, Del. My name is—"

"How the hell do you know who I am?"

"Well, if you'd hush up and get your finger out of my face," the petite brunette growled, the pupils of her eyes going from perfectly round to eerily elliptical in a single heartbeat, "I'd tell you that my name is Dr. Annabella Oleander St. Honoré and I went to school with Winifred Lightfoot-Blackthorne about a hundred years ago." She cleared her throat, almost immediately adding, "Well, not a hundred years ago, but some days it feels like it."

"Oh shit, I'm so—"

"Hush up. I'm not done."

Stepping back to avoid getting bonked in the chin as Annabella's hands flew all over the place, the apples of her cheeks flushing, Del had to work hard not to laugh out loud despite the situation. *"Well, you pissed that tiny fire salamander right off,"* Suri snorted. *"It's your special talent, Del, my girl. If opening your mouth and inserting both hands, both feet, and half a butt cheek was an Olympic event, you'd have the gold medal a hundred times over. You better say you're sorry sooner rather than later. 'Cause if she sets your ass on fire, imma lettin' it burn."*

"You wouldn't."

"Yes, I would," Suri sassed right back. *"I told you what would happen if you so much as singed a single sparkle on my beautiful—"*

"*Wings,*" Del finished with a groan. *"I remember. Please, dear Goddess, do not make me live through that again. I think I might—"*

Snap! Snap! Snap!

Annabella's fingers snapping right next to her ear pulled Del's attention back to the outside world just as the female fire salamander hissed, "Hello? Anybody in here?"

"I'm here," Del ground out through gritted teeth. "Now, if—"

"Like I was sayin'," Annabella scolded, not allowing Del a moment to finish her thought. Annabella was on a roll, and she wasn't about to stop until she said everything she needed to say.

"I like this girl." Suri chuckled. *"Yeah, for real, I like her a lot. She's got just the right amount of sass and spunk to be deadly in the best of ways. You better be nice. Who knows? She might just be Lady of Disaster number four. Of course, I'm not sure if the world's ready for you and Freddie and Dusty and Annabella to team up, but shit, who cares what they're ready for? Give 'em hell!"*

"Freddie and I studied biochemistry and biochemical engineering at Texas A&M so long ago I try not to remember. The second I laid eyes on that gangly tree frog, I knew there was gonna be trouble, and I was gonna love it."

Chuckling, the action softening her expression as much as her tone, the salamander went on. "She even hollered at me a couple of years back. Said there was a position at that FUCN'A place. I was just about to start teaching there when my momma and daddy suddenly passed away."

"I'm so sorry for your loss," Del quickly interjected, her heart literally hurting for her new acquaintance, knowing the pain that can come from losing your parents.

"Both you and your dragon can commiserate with that one." Suri sniffed. *"Breaks my heart that Kill and I have been the only parents y'all really have."*

"I don't think of you as a parent, dingbat ding dong. I still have Mom and Grandma, even though Daddy's already in heaven," Del grumbled. *"You, my pain-in-the-brain alter-ego, are more like a giant thorn in the left cheek of my—"*

"That's about enough outta you, Miss Missy."

"I could say the same." Del tried not to chuckle. *"Now hush it up. I'm tryin' to listen here."*

"Thank you, honey. It's still pretty fresh and hurt all the more because it was so sudden. Then things went from bad to worse. I couldn't take that job 'cause I needed to stay out here and take care of my brothers."

She batted at the air between them. "Don't get me wrong. I love those boys more than anything in the whole wide world. Family is everything to us. But let's be honest..."

Stepping forward and patting Del's arm, she winked. "We can only tell the men from the boys by the price of their toys, and my brothers are the worse. They can't be trusted as far as I could throw 'em, and I'm one strong fire salamander. Let me tell you. But that's not the point. We're still chasing down the danged culprit responsible for the death of our parents. Sucks even more that it's one of our own. The day I get my hands on hi—"

"The day *we* get our hands on Cletus," snarled a newcomer who seemed to appear out of thin air. A second fire salamander, this one giant, with flames coming out the tips of his fingers on one hand and icicles coming out of the other.

"Stop right there," Del ordered, spinning around so her bum was facing the intruder. Magic filled the air as she shifted—snapping, crackling, and popping like a metric ton of crispy rice cereal that had just gotten doused with just as much milk. The mysticism of her ancestors, along with one sassy-mouthed alter-ego, had the bottom half of her body instantly transforming. Lifting the last three sections of her long, thin dragonfly body, Del wiggled her cerci—the pointed tip of her tail—and snapped her head to the side.

Eyes boring into the monstrous fire—and maybe ice if they existed—salamander's eyes, she growled, "One more move, and you're dead. I'll fill you so full of venomous spikes that not even your momma will be able to identify the body, bucko."

Jumping between the pulsating end of her tail and the incredibly strange amphibian, Annabella threw her hands in the air and shrieked, "No! No! No! Stop! Don't shoot! This is my little brother Jeremiah! Don't hurt my baby brother!"

Backhanding the seven-foot-tall, red-skinned, muscled-like-Mr.-Universe-with-mismatched-hands salamander right in the chest, Annabella added, with no small amount of sisterly recrimination and a whole lot of love, "How many times have I told you not to scare people? You and our brothers are gonna be the death of me. I swear to all the little gators on the banks of the swamp, y'all just want to give me a heart attack."

Del narrowed her eyes while taking in the incredibly comical display before her, it all starting to make sense. And since that was a few more things than usually made sense, Del was thrilled.

Transforming back to 100 percent human, she turned around, still plenty pissed but needing clarification—like yesterday. Stepping forward and around Annabella, her finger pointing right at the end of her brother's giant amphibian-snubbed snout, she accused, "You're one of the salamander brother escapees, aren't ya?

"Well, yes, but—"

"Don't you *but* me. Imma 'bout to make a citizen's arrest. And while I'm at it, where the hell is Freddie?

What the heck and hootenannies did you do with her? Don't make me get crazy."

Another step forward—still pissed off and ready to fill the air with the hallucinogenic fog that only she and Suri could create with a special gland that just happened to be in their collective booty—the doc snarled, "'Cause if crazy's what you want, then you're pissing off the right girl."

"No, Del." Annabella once again jumped to her brother's defense. "You got it all wrong, girl. It was me." Beating on her chest with all four fingers of her left hand, as her big golden eyes got as big as saucers, the brown-haired shortie got louder and more adamant. "I mean. Yes, Jeremiah here escaped, but there's a good reason for that, too. What I mean right now is that I'm the one who zapped Freddie topside. There was a—"

"You. Did. What?" Snapping her head to the side, Del growled through gritted teeth. With her magic right back to pissed off, it popped and crackled all around her. She could feel Suri's wings threatening to burst out of her shoulder blades and her antennae real close to exploding out of the top of her head as her body turned the same way as her face, and she was nose-to-nose with Annabella. "How did you do that? We're locked down tighter than a nun's habit on Fat Tuesday in NOLA down here. There's no in, no out, no up, no down. Hell, I can't even get a call out to my mate. You gotta be crazy if you think—"

"No," Annabella snickered. "I'm not crazy. I just know where to look."

"You know where to what?"

"I know where to look."

Stopping short with her mouth hanging open, Del could only stare. Either Freddie's long-lost friend was out of her ever-lovin' mind or—, and this was a really big or—Del was dead and presently hanging out in the Great Inbetween. Aka shifter purgatory.

Not willing to accept that she'd died and was the last one to know, Del inhaled deeply, slowly exhaled, then asked, "So, where would you look, and what would you be looking for?"

"Well, it's a long story, but I'll make it quick 'cause Imma thinkin' we don't have a lot of time."

"I appreciate that."

"So, like I said, it was one of our own who killed our parents. Worse yet, it was Daddy's older brother, Uncle Cletus. Not only is he from the wrong side of the swamp, but the guy's crazy as a bedbug and thinks he can play God by giving the St. Honoré fire salamanders the power of ice, as well as flame."

"No shit?!" Del spat, the words flying out of her mouth as quickly as she thought them. The index finger of her right hand flying out to the side, just barely missing the end of Jeremiah's snout, she added, "Oh, I get it. That's why he looks like a giant Red Hot stuck in an ice cube tray."

"Hey!" the giant salamander yelped. "That's not cool."

"Hush, Jer," Annabella scolded before nodding at

Del. "Yep! He got caught by Uncle Cletus before the FUC agents got here. The other boys—"

"Jed and Jase," the youngest brother chimed in.

"Yeah, them." Annabella nodded, not missing a beat. "They were actually running toward that grizzly, your dragon, the honey badger who belongs to Freddie, and J.D. McAllen. We know them. Originally, the boys thought they could escape from the FUC jail, get back here to me, and we could stop Uncle Cletus." Shaking her head and blowing out a breath that made the thick fall of bangs covering her forehead rise and fall like feathers on a duck's butt, the female fire salamander lamented, "But that ship had sailed before the boys ever crossed the border. I just had no way to tell them to stay put. Ya know what I mean?"

"Ooookay." Del drew out the word, absolutely sure she'd fallen into an alternate universe where Annabella was the tour guide, Jeremiah was the horror show, and she was about to be the clown. "That still doesn't tell me where Freddie is or how you..." Raising her hands and making air quotes, she finished, "*Zapped her topside.*"

"Oh, that's easy." Annabella chuckled. "My great aunt twice removed, Beatrice, is actually Mama LuAnn." Nodding her head and smiling brightly like Del should know what that meant, the female fire salamander stood there for what seemed like forever but was actually less than three seconds.

The doc inquired, "And who, may I ask, is Mama LuAnn?"

"Oh, shoot." Annabella giggled. "The way Freddie talks about you, I was sure you knew everything, and I don't mean that in a snotty way. You have my undying respect. You, Dr. Del Weathersbee, are one smart cookie. I mean the best and the brightest I've ever read about, and that's sayin' somethin' because I've read just about everything ever written that has anything to do with biochemistry, biology, anatomy, physiology, and psychology."

"Thank you very much," Del gushed, feeling her cheeks heat with what she knew was a deep blush. "But Freddie's way smarter than—"

"Okay, all three of y'all ladies are the smartest of the smart," Jeremiah blurted out. "Einstein's got nuthin' on any of ya, but we really need—"

"*You need* to hush up, Jeremiah T. St. Honoré. Don't make me jerk a knot in your tail. I'm just about finished, and then we can go, ya hear me?"

"Yes, ma'am." He hung his head, abashed.

Del bit the inside of her cheek to keep from laughing out loud, her shoulders bouncing up and down as the tiny slip of a woman had her brother—in a massive salamander form that was at least twice her size—eating out of the palm of her hand in the blink of an eye. Had they not been in mortal danger, trapped at the bottom of a volcano in the middle of the Chihuahua Desert with a homicidal and totally psychotic fire salamander hellbent on making them his latest lab rats, it would've been the funniest thing the doc had seen in a long time.

Oh, hell, it was the funniest thing she'd seen since Hetty, the nurse at the FUCN'A clinic and Del's right-hand crow, had scared the crap out of Buck when he was trying to get a look at Freddie for the first time. Not only had the doc laughed so hard her sides hurt as it was happening, but she continued to tell that story to anybody and everybody who would listen, cackling like a loon the whole time.

"Anyway, like I was sayin'..." Annabella got right back on track. "Mama LuAnn St. Honoré is one of our kin. She just happens to be the best voodoo priestess in the whole of everywhere, and she taught me loads when I used to spend every summer with her."

"And that means?"

"Well, that means I used this here gris-gris bag..." Pulling a small purple satin sachet with bright green strings that smelled like dirty gym socks and cayenne out of the front pocket of her jeans, Annabella shook it in the space between them. "And a little Creole spell and located a tiny crack in the magical bubble Uncle Cletus has around us then added one helluva wallop of this."

Snapping her fingers, she conjured a blue and green flame that danced on the tip of her index finger. "And I sent Freddie topside with—"

"The whole danged gang," Jeremiah scoffed. "That grizzly bear, Miss Freddie's honey badger, the Sampson sister wolves, and three dragons. One of which is—"

"Oh, thank the Great Goddess," Del bubbled,

shaking her fists in victory. "But can I ask why I'm still here?"

"Oh, girl..." Annabella shook her head as her eyes filled with tears. "There just wasn't time. I tried—really, really tried. I wanted nuthin' more than to get you outta here, too, but Uncle Cletus sensed what I was doin' and shut that shit right down." Reaching forward, the petite brunette squeezed Del's shoulder. "But never you fear, we're gonna get you outta here and back with your dragon quicker than you can say sweet potato pie."

"It's okay," Del reassured, and she really meant it. "As long as Freddie and Matt are—"

Unfortunately, that was as far as the doc got, as an ear-splitting roar shook the volcano with such fury that lava rocks and dust rained down like hail on her head. Along with it came Matt's furious roar. "Where is my mate, you stupid red and blue gecko?! If you've harmed a single hair on her beautiful head, I'll skin your ass and wear your hide as boots."

Gasping at the sound of her mate's voice, Del was just about to scream her fool head off when Jeremiah huffed, "Well, hell. Looks like Cletus got your dragon, Doc." With his amphibian tongue adding a weird whispering lisp, he groaned, "Guess you're gonna wanna go save him, right?"

Chapter 6

"Answer me! Answer me, or I'll..."

Moving so fast he was nothing but a weirdly blinking blur of red and blue, the asshole who dared to jerk both Matt and Kill out of the sky flew from the other side of the cave the Guardsman was calling the Hole of the Ass. No matter how many years he lived or how many villains he had to take down, Matt would always wonder why every bad guy thought they needed a lair, and why said lair had to be underground.

And why did they always make a show out of moving from one side of that hole in the ground to the other? It wasn't as if they were being filmed or would even ever be immortalized in a comic book. The only answer Matt could come up with was that they were fucked up from the neck up.

Thoughts sped through his mind at top speed. Whether it was his worry for Del or his utter rage at the predicament he found himself in, Matt would never know. The only thing he could be sure of was that although a glowing red and blue, the bad guy in this chapter of his life was *not* Superman.

Of course, that led the Guardsman to ask himself, *how had a dickhead who couldn't hold his form been able to pull us out of the sky*? How dare he slam into the Guardsman like a ton of bricks and then some? Wasn't it bad enough that both of his salamander palms—one red hot and flaming, the other so cold Matt thought his bones might actually be frozen—attempted to rip the skin off the Guardsman's shoulders? Did the asshole have to hit the Guardsman's nose with his own snaggled snout with such force the cartilage cracked, and blood instantly flowed down Matt's face?

"You'll do what?" the asshole lisped, the tips of his forked tongue lapping up droplets of blood from Matt's face with a sick slurping sound that made the Guardsman's skin crawl. "Yep! You guessed it. Not a damn thing. You're stuck like a rat in my trap, Matthew Firestone. We're so far underground that not even those blasted MacAllens will find you, and here you'll sssure as ssshit ssstay until I'm good and done with your worthless hide."

"Says the asshole who can't hold his form for longer than a few sec…. ahhhhh fuck, shit, damn, son of a bitchhhhhhhhh!" Matt roared so loud that his own ears rang as the salamander kneed him in the crotch.

And from there, things got nastier than Zombie Day at Kill 'Em Dead Beach. Matt opened his mouth as wide as he could with every intention to give his captor detailed instructions for sticking his head up his ass. He was stopped when the amphibian jerked the entire top half of his body back as far as it would go.

Time seemed to stand still. Matt knew what was about to happen. Felt it in his bones. Could see it playing out in his mind. But there wasn't a damned thing he could do to stop it.

It was the proverbial train wreck he couldn't look away from. Sadly, Matt wasn't the locomotive. Hell, he wasn't even a bug on the windshield of the train. In the words of his old mentor, Matt Firestone was FUBARed with a snowball's chance in hell of coming out unscathed.

One sharp gasp of stale, nasty air was all he got before the stupid amphibian slammed himself forward with lightning speed. Blinding flashes of light ended in black dots dancing behind Matt's tightly closed eyes, followed by a headache the size of a horse's ass and then some.

Getting headbutted for the second time was bad enough, but with the incredible force of the back of his head hitting the wall behind him, things went from bad to worse. Not to mention the bits and pieces of hardened lava, rock, and sand flying in every direction.

That should've been the worst of it. If he'd had any luck at all, Matt would've passed out. But, *oh, hell, no!* Things went from bad to worse. The proverbial handbasket was well on its way to hell with no hope of a return trip when Matt realized his nose was so broken that it was completely flat to his face and hurt like a son of a bitch.

There was only one thing left to do – yell so loud the Devil himself might hear. "You stupid son of a bitch, asshole, motherfu…rarar rarraraaaarrrr…."

Still yelling past the foul-tasting hunk of cloth shoved into his mouth, Matt's eyes flew open, making his stomach jump into his throat and the half of a pound of honey-baked ham he'd eaten about an hour before attempt to make a hasty exit right out of his mouth. Refusing to be intimidated by the ostentatiously ten-foot-tall—and massively messed-up—fire salamander shifter, he gagged and spat until the stinky rag fell from his lips and he could cuss, "What the fuck is your problem? What do you want? Who are you? You have to be related to those shit-for-brains St. Honoré brothers. By the way, they're back in custody. So, you're shit outta luck, mutha fucka. Might oughta just give up before I—"

"Before you what?" The salamander snidely sneered. Taking a step back, he pointed to the slithering, inky black vines slinking out of the cracks in the floor and wrapping tightly around Matt's feet and legs and the massive manacles holding his uppermost appendages in place.

Fists clenched so tightly that the blunt tips of his nails punched holes in his palms, Matt jerked his arms up and forward, trying with all his strength—and a load of Kill's—to grab the neck of his captor. Arms suddenly flailing backward from the tension of the massive shackles and even bigger links of the chain connecting his hands to the walls, both his fists came rushing back like a freight train off the rails.

After a self-inflicted one-two punch and even more bone-crushing agony, he was forced to endure the raucous roar of Kill bellowing, *"What the hell is wrong with you? Do you have any idea how much magic it took to fix that ugly little nose of yours the first damned time? And let us not forget that that shit is at a premium down here. The fucked-up, messed-up excuse of a salamander you let knock us out of the sky is using—"*

"Voodoo," Matt hissed in unison with his Dragon King.

"Why yes." Kill chuckled. *"Damn, boy, I'm impressed. I thought we were past all that, but—"*

"But you're stalling because you have no idea how to counter whatever shit-ton of sorcery is flipping and flopping and whizzing around this cave. The messed-up excuse for a salamander may have just outwitted the once-great and always-boasting King Cillian."

"Now, hold on just one second," Kill growled. *"I didn't say—"*

"No, you did not, and that doesn't matter. You weren't gonna admit it no matter what I did or did not say. That's why—"

"Why you had to call me out about it, asshole."

"Wake up, loverboy." The salamander's slithering snarl was immediately followed by slaps to both sides of his face and a punch to the gut, which had Matt coughing out, "W-wh-what the fu-fuck was th-th-that for?"

"For you to pay attention," the salamander cackled, thunking the Guardsman's forehead with the heel of his hand so hard that the back of Matt's head hit the wall behind him for what seemed like the hundredth time.

"Either get on with whatever you're doing or put me out of my misery," Matt snarled. Pulling against his restraints and the vines making their fourth trip up and down his body, he ground out through gritted teeth, "My head is pounding like the drumline of a marching band, and the lack of circulation in my feet means they might fall off before my ass hits the floor. What the hell have you done with Del? What the fuck do you want? And do you want a head start?"

“A head start?” the salamander asked, looking confused, perplexed, and more than a little like a Picasso jigsaw puzzle with a couple of pieces missing.

"Yeah, doofus, do you want a head start when I get outta these fucking chains and come for your ass?"

"Oh, Matthew, Matthew, Matthew," the salamander *tsked*. "There will be no escape. There will be no head start. There will be nothing but your blood staining the floor of my laboratory as I rip the heart from your chest and chop it into little pieces." Stepping back, salamander moved an ominous black curtain to the side just enough for Matt to see a whole array of metal shelves and stainless steel carts filled with knives, scalpels, and saws and more than a few machines that *beeped* and *booped* in eerie syncopation. "Welcome to the lab, dragon ass. Now, I get to make you scream for your momma and wish you were never born."

Laughing out loud, unable to shake the feeling that he'd been kidnapped by the bigger-than-life, living, breathing embodiment of the neon sign over LuLu's Italian Ice Emporium in downtown Nonamesville, Matt knew he had a concussion. If Del were there, she would say his laughing was mainly because he was approaching delirium—and probably close to losing consciousness—but none of that mattered.

It was just too much. Not only had Matt's attempt to rescue his wonderful, fantastic, and terrific mate ended up with him being the one who was kidnapped, but the villain of his very own comic book story was flickering like a refrigerator bulb on the fritz. Blinking his eyes, trying to avoid the pop of glowing red accompanied by the harsh, bright white with an eerie bluish tint, Matt knew for sure that he was experiencing his first acid trip without the drugs. Not to mention flames jumped out the end of the salamander's fingertips one second and turned to icicles in the next. Not even Pink Floyd could make that shit up.

"Oh, my Goddess." Matt chuckled deliriously, the vision of his captor fading in and out of focus as his knees started to buckle, making everything absolutely hilarious. "You did this to yourself, didn't you? You fucked up some wild-ass experiment and turned yourself into a flasher. Hey! You could get a job as a traffic light at a four-way stop."

No sooner were the words out of his mouth than Matt was doused in what felt like a tidal wave of ice-cold water. Suddenly completely awake, dripping wet, and with his head feeling like a million little jackhammers were going to town on the inside of his brain, the Guardsman roared, "What do you want, Freak McFreakerson?"

"This!" the salamander roared, grabbing a set of shiny metal plates with oversized white handles and slamming them into Matt's chest. "This is what I want and what I'm gonna do!"

Filled with more electricity than he knew there could ever be flowing in the bottom of a volcano in the middle of the desert, the Guardsman felt his eyes roll back in his head as every hair on every square inch of his body stood on end. Eyes open so wide he was sure they would pop right out of his head, only the sound of Kill roaring, *"Don't pass out! Don't pass out! Don't you dare pass out!"* kept him from doing just that.

"Die, you stupid son of a bitch," the salamander shrieked, the ticking and popping noises of the opening and closing of the valves inside his flared nostrils getting louder with every ragged breath.

Spine straight, copious amounts of electricity quite literally lighting up his life, Matt wondered if he might be glowing. Thought it would be a nifty trick for parties where nobody would ever guess what he could do. Then the salamander jerked one of the paddles of the...

What the fuck is that?

"Defibrillator is the word you're looking for, lad," Kill snarled. *"Now, snap out of it and keep your damned eyes open. I just need to—"*

Before the Dragon King could get the rest of whatever he was saying out of his head and into Matt's, the Guardsman saw what his captor needed a free hand for and got as far as, "Don't you fucking da—" before the salamander spun the dial on the voltage regulator from barely registering to off the charts.

Shaking so hard his bones rattled and his insides contemplated turning to Jell-O, the pulsing of the minimal amount of magic Kill could muster just barely counteracted the electricity thrumming through Matt's body. And then he heard it—the most beautiful sound in the whole world. Music to Matt's ears! It was his one and only, sent from heaven via the Swamp dragonfly!

Del!

Damn it all to hell. He was happier than he'd ever been. She was alive! Yeah, she was cranky and giving somebody one hell of a piece of her mind, but Del was alive!

"And she's coming right toward us!" Kill and Matt roared in unison.

"You gotta stop her!" Matt begged his Dragon King. *"Don't let her—"*

"Keep the asshole with the paddle busy, and let me see what I can do."

"How the hell am I supposed to do that?"

"Talk to him, boy. Talk his ear off like you're always doin' to me. Dance a friggin' jig. I don't care. Just do what-

ever you have to so I can get enough magical mojo to reach Del before she lands in this pile of salamander shit right beside us."

"S-s-st… stop!" Matt roared, the sound rumbling over, around, and through him. "St-st-stop!" He couldn't help but stutter as the salamander only pushed the paddles harder against his chest.

"P-pl-please." Matt hated that he sounded pitiful and absolutely detested that he was begging, but this was Del's life they were talking about. He'd do anything and everything to be sure she was safe.

Opening his mouth to plead, to do whatever he had to do to get the bastard talking while Kill was… well, while Kill was doing whatever the hell he was doing, Matt didn't get so much as half a breath inhaled when his wonderful, fantastic, and terrific mate came running into the room wailing, "Let my dragon go, you big red, blue and blinking asshole!"

Chapter 7

Racing into the room, nothing else mattered but getting that flashing mess of red-and-black mottled skin and white-blue icy scales away from her mate. Del only half heard the bastard scream, "Attack," and worked hard to ignore Annabella and Jeremiah shrieking, "Watch out!" All of her attention was on Matt.

So, when she nearly ran into an entire gnarly wall of grotesque, wooly wasps not twelve inches in front of her face, Del screeched, "Holy shitcakes, what are these little fuckers doing in here? They don't like to be this deep underground. Why are there so many? Where did they come from? Why am I talking to myself?"

It was fascinating in the creepiest possible way. She'd studied the hawk wasps in college. Usually, solitary insects who burrowed in the side of mesas or deep into the sand, Del had only ever seen as many as ten hawk wasps group together, but there were at least a thousand floating in a big, black cloud right in front of her face.

Stepping back, with one eye on Matt and the asshole charging her mate up like a dead cell phone, Del peered into the center of their perfect formation. A mass like this one had to have a leader. Someone who spoke their language and called the shots. *There she is!*

Surrounded by all her newly adopted minions, rubbing their long, barbed tentacles together like thousands of evil geniuses with venom dripping from each of their deadly, long, sharp stingers, Del couldn't help but wonder, *Why are they hovering? Why aren't they attacking? What are they...?*

"The little assholes are waiting for you." Suri gagged. *"A horde of wasps with wings as sharp as daggers, lethal stingers on the tips of every single one of their nasty, hairy legs, and pinchers jutting from their homicidal mugs right under their millions of beady eyes, are waiting for you to tell them what to do. The minute you looked into their swarm, you, my dear, became their leader."*

"What the hell are they doin' that for?"

"Because I told them to."

"Because you what?!" She screamed so loud her ears were ringing, and her brain felt like it might explode. *"I do not have time for this bullshit, Suri. We have to—"*

"Save Matt," Suri yelled right back. *"Yeah, I know! So, make with the orders and get your minions to saving that hunka-hunka-sexy dragon-man of yours while I try to clear this voodoo bullshit outta the way."*

"But I thought Annabella and Jeremiah were gonna—"

"Yeah, sure, like I trust two salamanders to do a dragonfly's job. And don't tell me that Annabella knows voodoo. I know voodoo, honey. So, hush up and let me work."

"Okay, but—"

"Get the hell outta here, little lady," ordered the salamander, who was still forcing volt after volt of electricity into her gorgeous, handsome, and amazing dragon. "Get the hell out and give me back my wasps, or I swear I'll rip Matthew's head off right here and now."

"Fuck you!" Del roared at precisely the exact moment that Suri forced the shift with no warning or even the slightest heads-up.

Fully transformed, seven feet of mean-green and glittering-blue segments and four absolutely gorgeous sparkling wings, every cell bursting with the magic of those who'd gone before her, Del dispatched the wasps with a flick of her sparkly wing. Lifting off the ground with little more than a thought, she spun toward the salamander, thrust her wings forward and backward a single time, and dove straight for the heart of the blinking beast.

Dropping the paddles of the defibrillator, the stupid salamander ran one way, then the other, then back again, and ended up doing a strange kind of break dancing on the bent tip of his tail as the horde of hawk wasps bumped, tapped, and divebombed his head.

"Don't let him get away!" Del shrieked as Uncle Cletus bounced one way and the other, finally ending up on his feet just as Suri took control of their dragonfly form and rubbed their claw tips together.

Creating a strange melody only the wasps understood, Suri chuckled. *"See? I told you I should be queen. Those wasps aren't gonna let him get away, but they're not gonna sting him till you tell them to. Didn't figure a bad guy in the throes of anaphylactic shock would do us any good."*

"Good point."

Reasserting her control, Del landed on her back feet, mirroring Uncle Cletus' movements like she taught her students in Defensive Tactics 101. Closer and closer, she moved in, smiling as Suri whooped and hollered while Uncle Cletus looked like a deer caught in the headlights.

"Make a move, and I'll have those wasps sting your ass till it doesn't matter what color you decide to be."

"The hell you will," Uncle Cletus roared, running backward till he crashed into an unconscious Matt, who was hanging on the wall, impersonating modern art.

Grabbing a hunting knife off the stainless steel cart to his right, the blade Del hadn't seen until that moment, that blasted blinking salamander shoved his hands into Matt's hair and jerked his head up until the bones in his neck cracked. Slamming the blade against her dragon's neck, Uncle Cletus shrieked, "Call off those winged freaks and let me outta here, or I'll slit your man's throat and watch him—"

"No, you won't," Annabella shrieked, riding in on the shoulders of her now-flashing—not a great development—still-ten-feet-tall, still-stuck-in-salamander-form little brother. Tossing gris-gris bags like they were Mardi Gras beads and she was on the biggest float going down Bourbon Street, the petite brunette spewed a line of creole so long and so loud without taking a breath that Del was genuinely impressed.

Magic bounced from one corner of the cavern to the other. Sparks flew like fireworks on the Fourth of July. It was apparent that Annabella was trying to destroy the bubble of black magic her uncle had constructed, and even more evident that it was only about half working.

"No!" Uncle Cletus wailed, dropping the knife and running for the farthest corner of the galley-like cavern as his niece's uproarious spell casting and the resulting explosions irritated the hawk wasps almost as much as it pissed off Uncle Cletus.

Working all four wings double-time, Del curled the bottom half of her long, thin torso until she was shaped like a U, yelling, "Stop where you are, asshole! You're FUC'd!"

"You'll never take me alive!"

"Oh, my Great Goddess," Suri groaned. *"Time to bring in the big guns."*

Once again relinquishing control as her sassy alter-ego pushed her way to the forefront of their collective psyche, Del laughed out loud when Suri's voice came out of the dragonfly's mouth. "Hold it right there, Cletus, or I'm gonna pump you full of my special brand of venomous butt spikes."

Skidding to a halt, the blinking, flashing salamander's hand hit the wall to keep him upright as his head snapped to the side. "Screw you, dragonfly! Screw you!"

"No, dipshit!" Matt roared, the return of his magic along with Kill's flooding his system and curving his lips in a devilish grin. He shifted into his warrior dragon—a nine-foot, no-wings version of the airborne variety. In the blink of an eye, he took one huge standing long jump and landed right on Cletus' back. Shoving the heel of his massive paw into the back of the salamander's neck, he added, "Screw you, asshole. Show my mate some respect!"

Chapter 8

Refusing to get off the salamander even after Matt changed back into his human form, the Guardsman worked really hard not to laugh when Del got down on her hands and knees and lifted Cletus' head off the ground to ask him a few questions. It was even more hilarious when she inquired in a sweet, non-confrontational tone.

"What are you trying to do here, Mr. St. Honoré? What is all this about? Why did you experiment on yourself and your nephew? Just tell me what you did, and I'll do my best to change you back."

"Well, I had to try that crap on myself. She said it would turn me into some dino super soldier, but it didn't. When I tried to call her back, the number was dead. So, I had to try it again."

"She who?"

As if Del hadn't spoken, the old salamander—whose blinking and flashing had slowed to little more than an occasional blip—continued to answer the first questions Matt's mate had asked. "But I couldn't do it on myself again. I was already messed up and not getting any better. I needed somebody else, and well, hell, I couldn't try it on none of the other shifters out here. That's a sure way to get my head chopped off. It had to be family. So, when the boys called last week, I told 'em to come on home."

"You told them to escape?"

"Course, I did." He adamantly nodded, the movement making Matt feel like he was riding a salamander-shaped surfboard. "And they did it, too, didn't they?"

"Yes, sir," Del agreed. "They did."

"But then Jeremiah was the only one I could catch. Them other boys were just too danged fast. Had to be Jeremiah. After all, he was all I had. It couldn't be Annabella. My brother would've come back from the dead and kicked my ass if I bothered a hair on his little girl's head."

"Oh, come on, now," the petite brunette scoffed. Plopping down next to her uncle's head and crossing her legs like she was about to meditate, Annabella huffed, "Nobody's comin' back from the dead, and while I have your attention, what the hell's the matter with you? Did whatever you took drain your brain? You've always been one of the smart ones of the bunch. Damn, Uncle Cletus, you're losing IQ points by the second. You sound like Aunt Myrtle after a gallon of corn mash."

"I...I...ummm, Annabella?" Cletus' voice sounded tinny, almost breathy, completely the opposite of the maniacal psycho they'd been listening to up until that point. "I...I can't... I don't... It's just that... Annabella, is that you?"

Then he started to convulse, bucking and throwing himself around so hard that Matt was tossed off his back, flew through the air, and landed with a bone-jarring thud at least ten yards on the other side of the cave. Jumping to his feet, he raced across the cavern, one eye watching the salamander flopping like one big-ass fish out of water and the other on his mate who was trapped between said amphibian and a huge rock wall.

"Get the hell outta there, Del!" Matt bellowed. "Go! Run! That son of a bi—"

But it was too late. They had less than a minute, two at the most. He'd seen it too many times. That salamander was about to blow. Whatever Cletus had taken —the same shit that Zenobia had given to Alexander and the others—obviously was not compatible with the physiology of the St. Honoré family. Specifically, the "fire" in the fire salamander family.

"Grab your sister," the Guardsman barked at Jeremiah as he shifted into Kill's winged dragon. Wings tight to his side, it took him only a step and a half to get to Del, scoop her up in the talons of his shorter front paws, and throw her onto his back.

"Jump on!" he yelled to Annabella and Jeremiah, unfurling his wings as soon as he felt their weight on his back.

Following the map Kill was drawing in his mind, Matt rolled one way and the other, the tips of his wings just barely missing the long narrow passage of the tunnel walls as he made his way to the defunct magma chamber and the main vent leading topside. Whipping around one corner, then another, the first scent of fresh air tickled the Guardsman's senses.

One more corner and he would be there. One more right turn and Del would be safe. One more…

Boom!

"Oh shit!" Del's gasp filled Matt's mind. *"Was that…?"*

"Yep!" he confirmed before she'd finished her question. *"That was Cletus! Now, hold on, there's about to be—"*

Unable to finish his sentence as a high-pitched sound, reminiscent of the engine of Freddie's FUC-U 2.0, whooshed by, riding high on a gust of the hottest air he'd ever felt, Matt and Kill poured on the speed. It was all happening too fast. They weren't going to make it.

"Oh, hell, yes, we are," Kill growled through gritted teeth. *"I'll be damned if I'm dying in the bottom of some volcano in the middle of the desert!"*

"Here! Here!" Suri joined in, her magic filling not only Matt's heart and soul but Kill's at the same time. *"Take all you need. Just get us the hell outta Dodge, and in one piece!"*

"Me too!" came a smoky cheer before a wave of fiery enchantment joined the mix. *"Name's Sally. I just happen to be the salamander who shares a soul with Annabella."*

With no time for questions, Matt thrust his wings

forward and back with a strength unlike any other he'd ever known. Shooting down the final tunnel as if he'd been fired from a cannon, the air around them came alive. The mysticism of three super-bloodlines came together in an explosion rivaling the fireball barreling toward them.

"There it is!" Kill barked, his voice deep and rough. *"Shoot the loop and head for the top, lad."*

Dipping the tip of his snout until the bottom of the dragon's chin scraped the base of the magma chamber, Matt threw his huge head backward and headed toward the sky. No sooner had he and his passengers entered the main vent than the unmistakable hiss of friction and turbulence igniting the earth's gases whizzed by his head.

Racing toward the rays of the full moon, Matt's scales felt as if they were being ripped from his flesh as he broke through what little remained of the barrier of sorcery Cletus had used to hide his nefarious activities. The voices of his friends and family who'd remained topside burst to life in his mind, but there was no time to listen. He had to get them out of the line of fire, away from the tons of ash and lava that were coming their way.

"Get out of the way! It's gonna blow! The volcano's gonna blow! Get back! Go, go, gooooooo!"

Chapter 9

“Meanwhile, you bounced back nicely and put this little soiree together rather quickly,” Freddie chuckled.

“Yes, I did, and I do say so myself,” Del snickered, looking in the mirror to be sure her makeup was perfect.

“But if you tell me that flying out of the top of that volcano as it was erupting was a blast, I swear I’m gonna bop you in the head.”

"Hey, now." Del laughed out loud, winking at Freddie. "What have I told you about bopping me in the head?"

Hands in the air in mock surrender, the winged tree frog teased, “All right, no bopping, but you owe me a new plane.”

"No way." She shook her head furiously, trying not to laugh. "I did not make you crash your plane. You did that all on your own. Well, with the help of Cletus and his big, bad cloud of evil smoke. So, in other words, you, my friend, are shit outta luck."

"But you made us go all the way out there to that damned desert."

"Oh, no," Annabella chimed in as she entered the room, carrying a bouquet of the prettiest, long-stemmed red roses Del had ever seen. "It was you, Winifred Lightfoot-Blackthorne, who called me and said you were bringing your bestie to the desert for me to take a look at some contaminated blood sample."

"Yeah, well," Freddie scoffed, making Del bite the inside of her cheek to keep from laughing out loud. "That shit didn't work now, did it? Heck, we lost the blood sample before we even laid eyes on you, Annabella."

"Yes, you did, and, no, it did not," Annabella quickly responded. "But never give up hope. For all of Uncle Cletus' smarts, the man couldn't pick passwords to save his soul."

"So, you hacked him," Freddie cheered, made complete with a fist punch above her head. "Damn, I love you, Annabella."

"Love you, too, girl. And yes, I did hack that old fool. So, now we've got the notes that Uncle Cletus had before he blew up. The ones you said were from... umm...."

"Zenobia," Del and Freddie growled in perfect unison.

"Yeah, that crazy yellow jacket who tried to kill you and Buck, right?" The brunette nodded in Freddie's direction before turning back to Del. “And turned that dino your friend’s got the hots for into well… umm… a dino.” She chuckled. "Speaking of that, where is that Rhode Island Red and her man?"

"No clue." Freddie shrugged. "I asked Buck, and he didn't know either. He's gonna check with his mom to see if Dusty showed back up in the swamp."

"Well, that's good." Annabella nodded. "I just still can't believe that Zenobia chick caused all this mess just to create an army of super-soldiers so she could rule the world."

"Right?” Freddie agreed. "Do you think that's why your uncle took the bait and was carrying on Zenobia's work? Did he wanna rule the world, too?"

"Or just create an army of super-soldiers to have at his disposal?" Del added with a roll of her eyes and a shake of her head.

"I have no earthly idea on either account," Annabella huffed, shrugging her shoulders. "I swear insanity does not run in our family any more than anybody else's. Goddess only knows what Cletus was up to, I mean besides trying to create his own army and rule the world. Dumbass. Good thing dumbfuckery isn’t an inherited trait.”

Still shaking her head but with a smile returning to her face, the salamander confidently added, “I’m gonna find out everything my uncle did and everything he planned to do, and you can take that shit to the bank."

"And we'll be right there with ya," Del reassured. "You have officially been inducted into the Ladies of

Disaster, and that means we will always have your back come rain or shine or crazy relatives hellbent on world domination."

"Woohoo." the female salamander beamed. "I'm so happy to be here and thank y'all for giving Jeremiah that transfusion. At least he stopped flashing like a disco ball, and we're pretty sure he's not gonna explode. I admit that the boy makes my ass twitch, but I'm really glad he's not gonna blow up. Now, I just gotta get him back to normal so he can get back up to that jail and serve his time."

"And we'll be with you every step of the way," Freddie guaranteed. "But right now, Del's got a dragon out there just waiting to make her his."

"Well, hell," Del cheered, taking one last look in the mirror before getting to her feet and turning toward her friends. "Let's not make him wait any longer. I'd hate to get left at the altar."

Del had never felt prettier wearing an elegant, floor-length gown made of a cream silk and adorned with blue and green crystals along the neckline. Running her fingertips across the tiny red flames Hetty had meticulously embroidered, she took one final deep breath before walking out of their home and to the edge of the butterfly garden they'd planted together. It was absolutely perfect, everything she'd ever imagined her mating day would be, and so much more.

Standing just inside the white picket gate, Del's eyes went directly to the fountain in the middle of the garden just as Matt entered from the side. Dressed in a bright red surcoat like the Knights of the Round Table, her dragon was nothing short of breathtaking.

The light woven fabric matched the scales of his dragon, and the hem, neck, and shoulders were decorated with black corded trim. It made her giddy to think that she would soon be seeing firsthand what was under all those clothes as a mated woman.

Letting her eyes roam her mate's magnificent body, her gaze landed on the impeccable needlework adorning the material covering his chest. Unable to look away, she was astounded by the perfect depiction of Matt's dragon in the throes of battle, just as he'd been in that cave while battling Cletus.

Slowly making her way to the front of the garden, the thick crimson runner leading to the fountain warmed the bottom of Del's bare feet. Her heart beat double time, and her smile grew bigger the closer she got to the one man in all the world created for her.

When they talked about having a traditional Dragon Guard ceremony, and Matt had explained everything it entailed, she'd asked, "Now, how are we gonna do all that in Nonamesville, BC, with none of your people there?"

Of course, her dragon was quick with an answer, chuckling, "We're gonna do it like we do everything—together and our way."

And that was precisely what they were about to do.

Yes, they would be the only two attending the ceremony itself, but that was just fine with Del. After all, she was about to be part of the whole dragon world, so she might as well get used to their customs. Besides, she didn't need a crowd, and this way, she could be as goofy and ga-ga in love as she wanted, and no one would be the wiser. Then, later on in the week, after she and Matt had consummated their mating till their heart's content—and then some—their friends and his would host a full-blown reception.

Stopping next to her mate, Del's heart damn near jumped out of her chest. Every time she looked into his eyes, felt the touch of his hand, or inhaled the wonderfully smoky scent of her dragon, it was just like the first time, and she fell deeper in love.

The electricity of their connection skittered up her arms, flowed through her heart, and landed deep in her core. It warmed her from the inside out as Matt took her hands in his and gave a sexy rumble. "Hey there, pretty lady. You look gorgeous."

"Why, thank you, sir." She chuckled. "Ya don't look so bad yourself."

"Aw, you say the sweetest things, Dr. Delilah Flashwing Weathersbee Soon-to-be-Firestone. Whatcha say we get hitched?"

"I thought you'd never ask." She winked.

"Hold on, my love, here we go." Clearing his throat, Matt began to speak, the reverence of the moment making the air all around them alive with love and hope.

"Long ago, when knights and dragons fought side by side for king and country, it soon became apparent that dragonkin was no longer safe from those who would expose, exploit, and destroy them. Seeking to remain hidden and continue the Universe's mission to preserve not only their species but humankind, they sought to join with the knights who had so valiantly fought by their sides for so very many years. Thus, through magic and the will of both dragon and knight, the dragon shifters were born.

"In the infinite wisdom of the Universe and our founding elders, clans were set up, one for each color of the dragon kings whose soul we carry within our own. Each was assigned a region in which to make their home and to protect their families. Over time, some have flourished, some have ceased to exist, and others have been born from the joining of many. As the man blessed with the soul of King Cillian of the Cumhachdach Red Dragon Clan, it is an incredible honor to stand here today with the only woman I have ever loved or will ever love. Not only is she strong, independent, and a true mate for me in every way, but her soul is joined with Princess Surama of the Blue Empress Dragonflies of South America, giving her a strength that surpasses all others. Together, we will live our lives with the simple principle set forth by our ancestors at the beginning of time: keep the universe, family, and love at the center of our world, and none can ever come between us.

"I will spend every minute of every day of my life, Del, showing you how blessed I am to have you in my life. Like every dragon who finds the light of his soul, you, your health, and happiness are sacred to me, and I will forsake all others for you and only you."

"As I will do for you, Matthew," Del breathed, feeling the presence of the Great Goddess all around.

"Normally, the other Guardsman of my Force would be present to give their blessing, but since we have chosen to have an extraordinary ceremony for only us, my brother, Mason, recorded this blessing."

Pulling his phone from under his surcoat, Matt slid his thumb across the screen right before Mason's voice drifted from the speaker. "I, Mason Firestone, brother of Matthew and Dragon of Clan Cumhachdach, offer this blessing to one born of my blood and the mate of his heart. May their lives now and forever be a testament to all we hold dear…love, honor, and loyalty. As you are one, let your combined strength see you through many years, and may the children of your children's children smile upon you. May having your mate at your side be better than anything you've ever imagined. Just remember to keep your mouth shut and always answer Del with four very important words: honey, you're so right."

Laughing out loud, Mason's words making her even happier, Del winked at her mate as he said, "Honey, you're so right."

"Right back atcha, hot stuff." She chuckled.

Clearing his throat, Matt went on. "The witness and blessing of my one and only brother has been acknowledged, not only by myself but by my mate, the Universe, the Great Goddess, and the Ancients for whom we all—dragonkin and dragonfly alike—owe our very existence.

"The Red Dragons of Clan Cumhachdach were born of blood and fire. They are notoriously passionate in all areas of their lives. Their command and fierceness know no bounds, and their prowess in battle is uncompromising. The crimson of their scales symbolizes love and fertility. Cumhachdach Dragons will lead the charge, conquer the enemy, and defend our homeland and family with our very lives.

"To mate a Cumhachdach Dragon means to accept all that they are and honor the power that can only be shared between mates. May truth and honor always lie in your hearts and be the guiding light showing the way to what the other needs.

"As the bearer of the soul and the embodiment of the one true princess of the Blue Empress Dragonflies of South America, do you, Delilah Flashwing Weathersbee, take me, Matthew Firestone and my dragon, King Cillian, as not only your mate but the man with whom you will share your life?"

"With all that I was, all that I am, all I will ever be, and all that we are together, I accept you, Matthew Firestone, and all that you are into my heart and my soul. I will share everything that I am with you and Kill every day of our lives together, both here and in the Heavens."

Without so much as a second's pause, Matt answered, "For every day, rain or shine, fire or snow, day or night, with all that I am or all I will ever be, I pledge to love, honor, and cherish you, Delilah, and that sassy dragonfly of yours, Suri, for eternity and beyond. You will always come first, be the center of my focus and the love of my heart."

"Oh, Matt, I love you so much."

"I love you, Delly girl, and now, we will receive our mating marks, the outward representation of what we feel for one another."

Chapter 10

The longer she looked into his eyes, the deeper in love she fell with her dragon. Time stood still. Flames burst to life. Their hearts became as one, an affirmation of their lives, love, and their forever together.

Holding her breath as Matt lowered his lips to hers, Del nearly fainted as he stopped short and whispered, *"Ta' mo chroi istigh ionat."*

The gentle touch of his lips upon hers created an ache she never wanted to be without. It was an inkling of the magic to come, the promise of so much more burning deep within her soul. It was a spark, and their passion was the fuel. Spreading like wildfire, bursting to life in every fiber of her being, the flicker instantly became ablaze. It enveloped everything she'd ever been or would ever be, transforming her and her mate into one beating heart—one being—one everlasting love.

Opening entirely to one another, each bared all they were to the one person in all the world who completed them as no other ever could or would. Del felt their bond strengthening, solidifying, becoming the only lifeline either would ever need. Irrevocably connected, she was a part of him, and he was a part of her, just as destiny promised and fate demanded.

The world stopped on its axis. Del experienced Matt's feelings as if they were her own. She also knew beyond all doubt that her dragon shared her every sensation. A twinge on the left side of her neck was the only clue she got that she and her dragon had received their mating mark. Moving his lips across hers, Matt trailed hungry kisses across her jaw and nipped at her neck until he landed on the still pulsing spot. Licking and sucking until all thoughts of anything but their naked bodies loving one another vanished from her mind, Del's mate knew precisely what to do to set not only her but her dragonfly on fire.

Happily drowning in all that they were together, she objected with a soft moan as Matt reluctantly pulled his lips from hers, taking a hesitant step backward. Without a word spoken between them, he lifted her into his arms, held her close, and sprinted into their home.

Entering the master bedroom, Matt was utterly and totally shocked. He hadn't been back in the house since they'd gotten home from Texas, and he could see right away that Del had most definitely been busy. The room was transformed into the same space he always imagined he would share with his mate, right down to the solid mahogany, four-poster, California king bed in the very middle.

Decorated in the same rich crimson with black trim of his surcoat, Matt knew his mate had plucked the picture right out of his mind, and he couldn't have been more tickled. Pulling Del into his arms, Matt laid his lips to hers, kissing the woman made for him by the Universe with all the love in his heart and soul.

Moving her to their bed and making quick work of their clothes with no more than a thought, he picked Del up, gently laying her in the center of their bed. Sliding down her body, kissing and tasting every inch he could reach, Matt stopped only when his face was poised above the short, wet curls covering her pussy.

Nipping lightly, loving the way her skin blushed and her goosebumps got goosebumps, he continued to kiss the delicate skin all around as Del lifted her hips with impatient anticipation of what he'd promised would come. Inhaling her intoxicating scent, riding the high that only she could ever give him, the Guardsman chuckled against the inside of her thigh as her hands pushed into his hair, her nails scratched at his scalp, and she moaned, "Oh, my Goddess, Matt, are you tryin' to kill me?"

"Hold on just a bit," he teased. "I've gotta have a little feast before the main event."

Pushing his tongue through her sensitive lips, Del's indescribably wonderful taste burst to life in Matt's mouth. Lifting her legs over his shoulders, Matt made good on his word, licking her from bottom to top with the flat of his tongue, reveling as flashes of light exploded behind his eyelids, forcing him to go deeper. He needed more. Had to drive her utterly out of her mind. Needed her to never doubt that her pleasure would always come before his own.

Pushing one finger into her aroused flesh, he quickly added another. Thrusting in and out and driving her higher and higher, he separated her outer lips and drove his tongue as far as he could go with one smooth push.

Holding Del's hips as her back bowed off the mattress and her thighs tightened around his head, Matt smiled against her hot, wet pussy, more pleased than he'd ever imagined he could be at his mate's responsiveness to his touch. Making love to her with his tongue and fingers, he drew circles on her clit with his thumb. Placing his tongue flat on the bottom of her slit, Matt slowly licked from the bottom to the top to catch every drop.

On his second swipe, he sucked her engorged nub between his teeth and nipped lightly. Grinding her hips against his face, Matt's heart soared as he ate as if it were his last meal, knowing he could live on their love alone for the rest of his very long life.

Alternating between thrusting his tongue inside Del's pussy and licking her like she was the best ice cream cone he'd ever eaten, he refused to stop even when she pulled his hair with such force the

Guardsman was sure he'd be bald. But nothing mattered as much as pleasuring his sweet dragonfly, as making her happy, as being right where he was forever.

Licking her long and slow, determined to make Del scream his name over and over, Matt sucked her clit into his mouth and gently bit down on her swollen nub as he thrust three fingers into her body and curled the tips to reach her sensitive bundle of nerves. Coming with such force, the juices poured from her pussy, and he licked and sucked, sure to get every drop as Del's orgasms came one right after the other.

Petting and suckling her swollen lips, Matt felt his mate slowly return to earth. Smiling so wide that his cheeks actually hurt, he didn't even attempt to hide his overwhelming pride when she sighed.

"Oh, Matthew Firestone… I…I…"

"Yes, *m 'ionmhas*."

"That was… you were… oh, my Goddess," she whispered as her limp hand flopped across her eyes.

Overflowing with love, contentment, and gratitude for Del and that she was his, Matt let her legs slide carefully off his shoulders until they rested in the crook of his arms. Kissing up the inside of her leg, across her hip and her stomach, he positioned his cock against the swollen, flushed lips of her pussy, rubbing the head slowly against her clit where it peeked out of its hood.

Coating himself with her juices, he slowly pushed into Del, stopping only when the head of his cock lay just inside. Each clutch, every contraction pulled him deeper inside, making breathing almost impossible and making his heart race like he'd just run up the side of a mountain.

Gritting his teeth as he pushed forward inch by glorious inch, Matt teased them both until their panting echoed through the room and sweat ran down his spine. Stopping when he could go no farther, the Guardsman held perfectly still, savoring the feel of his mate's hot body massaging his pulsing cock.

Erection growing even harder, Matt had no doubt that the top of his head would blow right off if he didn't soon come, but he refused to hurry. This was the first time he and Del were together in their home as a mated couple, in their bed, safe and sound, and it was meant to be savored.

He dreamed of staying buried deep inside her forever, held together by the perfect union that only happened when true fated mates came together. Unfortunately, if he didn't move soon, Matt was going to explode like a randy teenager and embarrass himself with the only woman who would ever matter to him.

Slowly pulling out of the heaven of his Del, the Guardsman hovered at her opening. The slightest movement would have caused him to slip from the only place he ever wanted to be. Pushing forward, he watched his throbbing cock disappear into her warm, wet pussy. The sight of them joined as one, as was always intended, caused Matt's balls to draw up close to his body and his eyes to cross.

Increasing their rhythm, each stroke of Matt's cock

rubbing against Del's feminine walls, his gaze wandered along the gorgeously erotic curves of his dragonfly. She was all woman and all his. He marveled as her large, full breasts bounced with each bump of his hips against hers. His mouth watered as he remembered the taste of those deep, rose-colored nipples.

Leaning forward, he palmed her breasts, bringing her knees, which were still draped over his arms, as far forward as he could. Rolling her nipples between his thumbs and forefingers, Matt was instantly rewarded with his name tumbling from her lips in a low, slow mantra.

With her legs bent higher, he could sink deeper into his mate, feeling an unparalleled closeness with the woman who held his heart and soul within her own. With his cock buried to the hilt in his delectable dragonfly, he swiveled his hips, bumping her clit with every movement and driving every intelligent thought he ever had right out of his mind.

Thrashing her head side to side, held captive as Matt used his whole body to tease her to a frenzied peak, Del looked like a true goddess. Her long mane of red curls flew like her very own wings as she chanted his name, the last coming out as a scream to the Goddess. "Matt… Matt… Matt… Matthew!"

"Hold on, *mo gu bràth gaol*," he grunted through gritted teeth, barely holding back his own climax. Lifting her legs just a fraction, he practically begged as he panted, "Look at us, *mo ghrá*. Joined together as the

Goddess intended. Loving one another now and forever."

Eyes snapping open, Del's gaze flew to where they were one. Smiling as she watched him take long, deep strokes in and out of her, Matt couldn't hold back any longer. Grinding his pelvis against her clit, the Guardsman held perfectly still as his mate screamed her release, "Yes! Yes! Yes! *I love you, Matthew*!"

Falling into the endless chasm of their love, as Del's body squeezed his cock, Matt roared, "And I love you, Delilah Firestone! With all my heart and then some!" as he emptied himself into her.

Matt held on for dear life as their climax went on and on. When her pussy's hold on his cock began to relax, he moved in and out of her shaking body with slow short strokes, bringing his sweet dragonfly back to earth and allowing both their racing hearts to return to normal.

Legs shaking from exertion, his heart so full of love he knew he could have died right at that moment, Matt lovingly pulled Del to his chest. Rolling and twisting, he landed with his back on the bed, and his miraculous mate draped across his sweat-soaked chest. Fingers trailing up and down her spine, he simply enjoyed the silkiness of her gorgeous skin.

Time meant nothing as long as he had Del in his arms, so when she opened her eyes, lifted her head, and asked, "What time is it?" Matt could only shrug and chuckle. "I have no idea."

No sooner were the words out of his mouth than the doorbell rang. "Who the hell…"

Up off the bed, Del pulled Matt's T-shirt, so big it fit her like a dress, over her head then wagged her finger in his direction. Rushing out of the room, she hollered over her shoulder, "Don't you move a muscle, Mr. Firestone."

Thankfully, Del was back quicker than Matt had expected and carrying a big brown bag with handles. Sniffing the air, Matt smiled. "I know what's in that sack."

"Yeah, but you cheated." Climbing up onto the mattress, she began to unload honey baked ham, honey yeast rolls, and two honey pecan pies from none other than Sam's Diner in Valentine, Texas.

"Hey, how did you get that here? And it's still steaming hot. I know the Sampson sisters don't deliver, especially two thousand miles."

"I might just know a certain lady fire salamander with the power of a voodoo priestess and the phone number to those very same Sampson sisters."

Crooking a finger as Del chuckled, Matt purred, "Come over here for a second and let me show you how much I appreciate you."

Loving that she trusted him enough to do what he asked without question or reservation, Matt pulled Del into his lap as he reached into the pocket of his jeans, which he'd retrieved while she was out of the room. Kissing her soundly, he leaned back and said, "Hold out your hand."

When she did it, he slid a four-carat ruby ring on her ring finger. He was happier than any man had a right to be when she squealed in delight, hugged him, kissed him, and gushed, "Oh, my Great Goddess in green go-go boots, Matthew Firestone, when did you have time to get this?"

"Well, I might have had it since the first day I met you, and I might have just been saving it for this very occasion."

Kissing him soundly, Del beamed. "And I might just be the luckiest dragonfly doctor in the whole damned world."

"Nah, it's me who's lucky." He winked. "Now, give me that hand back if you don't mind."

Smiling from ear-to-ear as she once again held up her left hand, Matt slipped his mother's wedding band alongside the ring he'd had made for her. Looking at the exquisite diamond eternity band—a perfect circle to symbolize their never-ending love—the Guardsman fought back tears. He wished his parents could meet Del. There was no doubt in his mind they would love her just as much as he did.

Raising his eyes, not surprised at all to see the tears in Del's eyes, he teased, "Those better be happy tears, Mrs. Firestone, or else I might have to get tough with you."

"They are." She sniffed, holding up her hand. "And these are just so gorgeous. Are you sure you want me to have them? It's so… so… so amazing. I know these stones mean something to your clan, and maybe Mason should have at least one of them."

"Oh hush," Matt playfully scoffed. "Let my brother get his own rings if and when he ever finds a mate who can put up with him. These are yours. My first memory of my mom is her showing me her ring and telling me that someday my mate would wear it. She would be so proud."

Wrapping her arms around Matt's neck, his dragonfly showered butterfly kisses all over his cheeks before pulling back and, with a straight face, asking, "Aren't you forgettin' something?"

"Umm…. I don't… think so." Words trailing off, the twinkle in Del's eyes getting brighter, he added, "What are you up to?"

Grabbing the biggest honey yeast roll out of the Styrofoam container, the one right on the top, Matt watched intently as Del gently tore the soft sweet dough in two and pulled out a perfect platinum wedding band. Lifting his ring finger before she even asked, he chuckled as she slid it on and winked. "Great minds think alike, huh, Mr. Firestone?"

"They damned sure do, Mrs. Firestone," he agreed in between peppering her lips with kisses. "They damned sure do."

The End.

Or is it? Because there's a certain Rhode Island Red

Hen who's still waiting for her HEA! Stay tuned for *Dusty and Her Dino*, coming soon!

And there are more FUC Academy books from other authors coming your way!

To find out more about these books and more, visit Worlds.EveLanglais.com or sign up for the EveL Worlds newsletter. If you haven't already downloaded the **free Academy intro** (written by Eve Langlais) make sure you grab it at worlds.evelanglais.com/wordpress/book/fucacademy1!

DRAGON KIN LANGUAGE INDEX

DOC AND HER DRAGON: GAELIC

Mo Chroí..........My Heart

M 'ionmhas..........My Treasure

Fìor bhuille mo chridhe..........The very beat of my heart

Ta' mo chroi istigh ionat..........My heart is within you

Mo gu bràth gaol ....*My forever love*

ALSO BY JULIA MILLS

A Tree Frog and Her Honey Badger

The world has gone mad! Absolutely nuckin' futs crazy! Well, maybe not yet, but Dr. Winifred—please call her Freddie—Lightfoot is sure all hell's about to break loose if she doesn't stop the idiot who's destroying the world's coffee fields.

Life without caffeine is a no-go for this FUC superhero. A world without her favorite drink is not a world she wants to live in. Time to throw on her rainbow wings and kick tail, even if it means putting off meeting a certain sexy-as-the-day-is-long honey badger.

Retirement was boring. Buck Blackthorne needed adventure, purpose, and to be on the front lines again. One quick email to Furry United Coalition Newbie Academy—FUCN'A—and everything was a go.

With more years of combat under his belt than all the cadets combined, he just knew training would be a snap! Well, like a bang, boom, kapow and a trip to the infirmary… on second thought, maybe retirement wasn't so bad.

But one whiff of a certain sexy winged tree frog and all bets were off. He was in for the long haul and ready to claim her as his own… But where the hell did she go?

One unanswered phone call, a supersonic trip south, and jumping from a perfectly good plane was all in a day's work for this honey badger hero. There wasn't a jungle that could stop him, but prehistoric shifters? Well, that was a new one.

Time to save his mate, save the day, and, heaven help him, save the coffee! Oh, baby, put your head between your legs and kiss your booty goodbye. Time to get FUC'd in the best possible way.

Available now on all platforms!

Doc and Her Dragon

A dragon king and a dragonfly take on an icy-hot salamander in this next addition to the FUCN'A world!

Take one doctor with a glittering green body, sparkly wings, and a sassy alter-ego who refuses to take no for an answer. Add an explosives professor with red scales and a heart of gold who shares his soul with an ancient dragon king.

Mix in the most FUCN'A band of amazing friends a couple could ask for, and you've got a story like no other that will have you laughing, cheering, and falling in love till the very end!

Doc and Her Dragon are out to solve the conundrum of a seriously deranged and absolutely deceased megalomaniac and psychopath who is posthumously trying to turn the shifters of the world into super dino super soldiers.

Stop right there! You're about to be FUC'd—in the best possible way, and that's just the beginning!

Available now on all platforms!

Dusty and Her Dino

Coming Soon!

Also in Julia's Dragon Guard World:

Read Ranger's story in *Dragon Falling* and J.D.'s story in *Save a Horse, Ride a Dragon*. And if you want to read about

the creation of the magic crystals that Del and Freddie were after, check out *She Thinks My Dragon's Sexy*!

ABOUT JULIA

Julia Mills is the *New York Times* and *USA Today* Bestselling Author of the Dragon Guard Series. She admits to being a sarcastic southern woman who would rather spend all day laughing than a minute crying. She lives with her two most amazing daughters and a menagerie of animals, which keeps her busy, but not so busy that she can't make time to tell a good story!

Julie believes that a good book, along with shoes, makeup, and purses, will never let a girl down and no hero ever written will compare to her real-life hero, her dad! She's a sucker for a happy ending, and alpha men make her swoon.

Website: juliamillsauthor.com
Newsletter sign-up: eepurl.com/gc2ALP
Facebook group:
facebook.com/groups/1428602220788961

facebook.com/JLakeMills
twitter.com/JuliaMills623
instagram.com/juliamills623
pinterest.com/juliamills623
bookbub.com/authors/julia-mills
goodreads.com/7200721.Julia_Mills

www.ingramcontent.com/pod-product-compliance
Ingram Content Group UK Ltd.
Pitfield, Milton Keynes, MK11 3LW, UK
UKHW040009200726
13854UKWH00001B/107

9 798201 720544